Classic
Golf
Clangers

Classic Golf Clangers

David Mortimer

ROBSON BOOKS

First published in Great Britain in 2004 by Robson Books,
The Chrysalis Building, Bramley Road, London W10 6SP

An imprint of Chrysalis Books Group plc

The author has made every reasonable effort to contact all copyright holders.
Any errors that may have occurred are inadvertent and anyone who for any
reason has not been contacted is invited to write to the publishers so that a
full acknowledgement may be made in subsequent editions of this work.

British Library Cataloguing in Publication Data
A catalogue record for this title is available from the British Library.

ISBN 1 86105 743 1

Typeset by SX Composing DTP, Rayleigh, Essex
Printed by Creative Print & Design (Wales), Ebbw Vale

Contents

Classic Golf Clangers

This book is dedicated to all those happy hackers who keep the golf industry buoyant by losing roughly 32,500,000 golf balls every year in Britain alone. That amounts to about 26 missing balls per person per year, so it's just as well for the unemployment figures that the 'unloseable' golf ball, invented in 1937, never caught on.

The author has much for which to thank the British Newspaper Library in helping to flesh out detail or jog the memory. He has also had inspiration for one or two pieces from certain books that, if any golf fan has not yet read, he thoroughly recommends: Peter Alliss's *Golf Heroes*, Norman Dabell's *Winning The Open* and Don Wade's *And Then Jack Said to Arnie* . . . and *And Then Arnie Told Chi Chi* . . . Finally, my late father-in-law, Dr A C Gordon Ross, who loved the Old Course at St Andrews, however many times it defeated him, bears the major responsibility for the tale of 'Admiral Benson's Bunker'.

Foreword

'In his case,' said Mark James, commenting on a pro who had better remain nameless, 'there will be far more days when he will hit the middle of the fairway rather than the centre of an oak tree. It just shows that in golf, as in life, you simply don't know what's around the corner.' There indeed is the rub for the golfer, or the player of any sport that is wholly dependent on individual performance. You can never escape the unblinking eye of the spectator or of your playing partner, nor the all-seeing camera lens.

In a team sport such as cricket there are times when you stand out from the crowd, and there is no shortage of opportunity to make a complete prat of yourself by, say, padding up to your first ball and being bowled. But at least you can escape back into the ranks of your team. You may have failed dismally, but the rest of them will rally round to put things right and you'll repay the debt next day, or next month. Golf offers no such relief. You're on your own, subject to all the mental pressures that a double bogey can impose or the anxiety of watching your lead drain away as each bunker shot drives the ball ever deeper into the sand. Short of hiring a sports psychologist to caddy for you, there's no one to offer a comforting shoulder or a helpful hint.

What is our role as onlookers in adding to this pressure? Taken individually, each of us is no more than a small digit, collectively adding up to the millions that comprise a TV audience for a great event such as the British Open. The more of us who switch on, the more money the TV companies shell out for rights and the more advertisers wish to be associated, so in the end the golfers may be playing for well over a million dollars. That makes for plenty of pressure. As spectators, we take sides, rooting for one or other of the contestants. When our man or our woman wins, we celebrate him or her as a hero, whether it's Sandy Lyle winning the Masters or Paul McGinley holing his putt to secure the Ryder Cup, and chronicle them accordingly. When X, Y or Z fluffs an approach shot, we may clutch our heads and groan in sympathy – or something worse – but only occasionally do we heap opprobrium on the unfortunate player. It could all too easily have been us.

One of the great attractions of golf, as in any sport, is the interplay of human skills and emotions that it displays, and the way the participants rise or, sometimes, fall to the occasion. As Mark James says, you don't know what's around the corner. The fates that have just dropped an eagle into your lap may choose to have a giggle when your next drive ricochets off a branch to finish fifty feet behind the tee. I know. I've done it (but without the benefit of the eagle first).

This little book celebrates some of golf's red-faced moments drawn from 120 years or more of its history, and while it certainly puts names to the blushing faces, be they of players, caddies or officials, it has absolutely no desire to shame them. Not only have most of them suffered enough already, but they were generally giving their all when the clanger was dropped, and in most cases those very same individuals provided us with many more hours of pleasure than of cursing. Affection with, maybe, some occasional gentle humour is the order of the day!

James IV Mistakes Flodden For a Golf Course

The beginnings – how golf came to be, Scotland, 1502

It was the Scots who invented golf, despite efforts by insensitive Anglo-Saxons to try to find its origins elsewhere. The Dutch had something called Kolf, which involved hitting a ball towards a distant post, but, as the ball was the size of a cricket ball and the club more like a hockey stick, it's safe to assume the Dutch were groping after cricket (or possibly hockey) and, having failed to invent either, they forgot about Kolf.

No, it has to be the Scots for at least two unanswerable reasons. First, all along the sandy east coast they had this infertile land linking (hence 'links') the seashore and the cultivable acres inland. It was a pity to let it just sit there, especially with sheep nibbling the grass in the hopes you'd spot that they were creating fairways, so using it for golf was the obvious solution. Secondly, the Scots have spent a great part of their history either fighting each other (popular) or finding ways of putting it across the English (easier, and therefore massively popular).

The man most often credited with forcing golf upon a willing population is James IV, who is known to have placed an order with his club maker in 1502 in preparation for a match against the Earl of Bothwell. No doubt he was planning a tournament in which the flower of Scottish nobility would thrash the English 10 and 8 but, unwisely, he lost patience – perhaps under pressure from those in his court who were having trouble getting their handicaps down – and dropped the first great golfing clanger by taking an army over the border instead.

In 1513 he and his army dropped the second clanger when they landed in a hazard called Flodden and were dispatched to the great golfer in the sky. This left his daughter Mary, Queen of Scots, to chip out of the rough single-handed and, as far as we know, establish herself as the first lady champion in golfing history, despite once losing to one of her own attendants called Mary Seton. Rather sportingly, Mary (QoS) gave her a necklace to wear round the neck she might well have severed had she been in that kind of mood. My own belief is that John Knox's outburst against the 'monstrous regiment of women' was, in reality, provoked by finding that Mary and her ladies-in-waiting had bagged all the best teeing-off times at St Andrews when he had been looking forward to a boisterous round with his pals.

Mary passed the family enthusiasm for the game on to her son, James VI, and when he found himself travelling south to London to become king of England in 1603, he took care to pack his clubs. Suddenly the English realised golf was a Good Thing, and founded the Royal Blackheath Golf Club in 1608 (or maybe 1766, but why let the evidence and a mere 158 years spoil a good story?).

For the next two hundred years or so, aristocrats and gentlemen amused themselves with the game as a pretext for getting out of the house and eating and drinking vast quantities, the preferred tipple being claret. This liquid medium was frequently used as the currency for wagers on contests (hence the Auld Claret Jug was the trophy awarded to the winner of The Open). The men who carried the clubs for the gentlemen players, and made their clubs and featherie balls for them, were the professionals and, little by little, they began to come to the fore as performers in their own right.

The very first Open was held in 1860 to determine the best golfer in Scotland, and therefore the world, upon the sudden death of Allan Robertson, who had hitherto been accepted as the best because he said so. There were eight participants, all professionals, so strictly speaking it was not an open tournament at all, as was reflected in the prize – a measly red morocco belt. For a decade a variety of people called Tom Morris won The Open with monotonous regularity – there was Old Tom, who won four times, and there was his son, Young Tom, who also won it four times, three of them in succession, which meant he got to keep the belt and enjoy a big saving on braces. Since amateurs had by now muscled in on The Open, it seemed appropriate to replace the prize of a belt with that of a claret jug – and Young Tom won that as well, dammit!

Dinna Cleek Yer Featherie at Me, Mon

Golfing equipment takes a few little hops forward, 1870s–1938

The Victorian passion for tidying things up and organising them, combined with the slow but steady distribution of greater leisure time and spending power, meant golf could now begin its progress, stately at first, towards becoming one of the world's most popular sports. The expansion of the market meant that more time and experimentation were expended on the playing equipment. First in line for tinkering was the ball.

In the bonhomie of the bar you have probably remarked on the number of top hats to be seen in early Victorian photographs. In my local they talk of little else. The explanation, once you know it, is disarmingly simple: the wearers were golfers who made their own balls. For over two centuries golf balls were made of feathers, and for one ball you required a precise top hat full of goose or chicken feathers. Clearly, therefore, it was expedient to carry your measure with you so that you could relieve a passing goose or chicken of the necessary quantity of feathers before rushing home, soaking them, stuffing them into a leather outer case and stitching it up.

It was slow work, mind you. Even someone as skilled as the great Scottish golfer of the 1850s, Allan Robertson, could produce only three a day, and the price was accordingly high – around four shillings, which today would be worth more than £25! A good golfer could dispatch a 'featherie' between 150 and 200 yards but, if he topped it, it was liable to burst with a spectacular effusion of feathers, and that was another £25 down the drain. Modern apologists tend to denigrate Britain's imperial expansion in the nineteenth century, but it had one beneficial side effect because, from Malaysian tree resin came the gutta percha, or 'guttie', ball, whose casing was marked and indented to produce better flight. The guttie ruled for half a century until the Americans got in on the act and produced the modern wound ball. Queen Victoria could thus expire peacefully, secure in the knowledge that the future of golf in her dominions was assured.

In the days of the featherie, the clubs were made of wood and were generally called spoons. And why not? On the rough bumps and hillocks of the links, spooning the ball up, over and round was the best way to go, so there were long spoons, middle spoons and short spoons, not forgetting the baffy spoon with its laid-back face, which could loft the expensive featherie with little fear of splitting it. The only iron club a golfer would carry would be a sand iron. Even the putter was made of wood, generally with a deep head for biffing it across the rough, uneven greens.

As the 1890s progressed, iron clubs gradually began to replace many of the woods until only the driver and brassie (so called because of the brass plate screwed to its underside to protect it when playing off rough ground) were left. There were driving irons and lofting irons (even rutting irons – not, alas, for players with the libido of stags in autumn but for getting out of, well, ruts), not to mention mashies, spade mashies, niblicks, mashie niblicks, pitching niblicks and the never-to-be-forgotten cleek, which the Lord has not, alas, preserved outside museums.

According to Malcolm Campbell, in his *Encyclopaedia of Golf*, the mashie was a 'short-headed, heavy club of iron' that lofted the ball for short approach shots – approximating, in other words, to a 5-iron. The magnificent cleek, on the other hand, was a 'driving mashie', or an iron of medium loft for long approaches, a 1- or 2-iron. How very romantic it all sounds! The thought of Harry Vardon, who won his record sixth Open in 1914, studying the lie and saying to his caddy, 'The wind's in the wrong direction for the cleek – I think I'll take the mashie here and lay up just short of the bunker' makes one regret the mathematical precision that nowadays condemns us to woods and irons numbered precisely from 1 to 10. Even a forgiving man might call this wilful desertion of the cleek and the mashie a clanger.

The malign progression towards unromantic numbers was started on its downward journey by the introduction of the golf bag in the 1880s leading, as it did, to a proliferation of clubs, two-thirds of them unnecessary. When you or your caddie had to stagger round the course carrying under your arm what Winston Churchill once called 'weapons singularly ill-designed for the purpose', you found you could play wonderful golf with remarkably few clubs.

Once the bag appeared, the number of clubs inside it grew like Topsy, exceeding thirty in some recorded instances. Presumably, the more clubs you carried, the more security blankets you felt accompanied you (which suggests my heroine, the splendid Gloria Minoprio – see page 27 – must have been a very self-assured young woman). Finally, fearing the introduction of a horse and cart to carry a golfer's equipment, the US and British authorities decreed in 1938 that the maximum number of clubs a tolerably well-adjusted golfer could possibly need was fourteen, for which relief caddies ever since have doubtless given nightly thanks upon their knees.

That's Not How We Do Things Here, Old Boy

The British Amateur Championship, Royal St George's, 1904

Having invented the game, the Scots very naturally believed they owned it and, just to prove the point, a Scot won the British Open for every one of its first thirty years until John Ball interrupted the procession in 1890. This was disconcerting until it occurred to them that they could colonise the old enemy by spreading the game southwards – the first Open held in England was in 1894 – while remaining in firm control of the rules. In 1897 the Royal and Ancient in St Andrews therefore became the governing body for the game everywhere in the world (and it still is, barring only the USA and Mexico). This tactic for keeping the English under control worked, on the whole, very well and allowed everyone a comfortable inner glow since, in a manner of speaking, it kept everything in the family.

Once it was clear who ran the show, it became all right to encourage the Americans, and British players would venture across the Atlantic from time to time, to win everything in sight and either come home well rewarded, or stay over there to teach, build courses and so on, and be even better rewarded. This was fine while it lasted, but in the Edwardian age there began to be disturbing signs that Americans were getting rather good at the game. Quite a number started coming to Britain to take part in competitions, and that was tolerable so long as they didn't win. But, when one of them broke the unwritten understanding and

7

walked off with the British Amateur Championship of 1904, it was considered jolly unsporting.

Walter Travis arrived as three-time winner of the US Amateur and was considered unbeatable with a putter in his hands, so his opponents were not unduly dismayed when, during his preparations for the championship, he couldn't find his touch on the greens.

'Can't cope on British links, old boy. Always said so.'

But Mr Travis was carrying a secret weapon in his bag and, when it was time for the competition proper, he brought it out. It had much the same effect as a sub-machine-gun might have had at the Battle of Agincourt. It was a Schenectady putter, so-called from the city in New York State in which it was made. It had a mallet-shaped head and a central shaft, and with it Mr Travis not only disposed of some testing putts but also, with ease, of some notable opposition. He knocked out H H Hilton, twice winner of the Amateur and twice Open champion; then he dispatched Horace Hutchinson, who had won the Amateur in 1886 and 1887; and in the final he beat Ted Blackwell 4 and 3, despite being consistently outdriven. His triumph was received with – how shall we put it? – foot-shuffling and throat-clearing.

The problem was that, although Travis's magic putter was kosher according to the US Golf Association, St Andrews had not got round to thinking about it and could not, therefore, find a legitimate way of expressing their disapproval other than blowing their noses rather loudly. Even so, it took them six more years to ban the Schenectady. Forty years later they un-banned it – and Ben Hogan was using one when he won the 1953 Open at Carnoustie.

Foredoomed to Failure

George Lyon remains Olympic champion, 1908

You would be hard pressed to explain how golf came to appear on the Olympic menu. However careless it was of them, the ancient Greeks had not got round to inventing the game by the time their empire faded away and the Games ceased; and, when Baron de Coubertin restarted the Olympic idea in 1896, golf was not at the top of his must-have list.

On the other hand in those far-off, prewar days of wealth and leisure, just about all organised and semiorganised sport was in the hands of gentlemen amateurs, and any excuse for a sporting shindig was good enough for them. Arnold Jackson, for example, may have been a bit grumpy about abandoning his fishing trip to Norway in order to run in the 1,500-metres race at the 1912 Stockholm Games, but he pottered along all the same and beat a strong field to claim the gold medal. So, logical or not, golf was one of the 21 sports to be staged during the British Olympics, and the 1904 champion, Canadian George Lyon, was quite willing to come and defend his title in 1908.

Strictly speaking, these were not British Games, but English ones, the official venue being London. The arrangements for staging the golf and for the overall organisation, therefore, fell to Ryder Richardson, the secretary of the Amateur Championship Committee as well as of Royal St George's GC. This did not meet with the approval of the Royal and Ancient in St Andrews, who regarded themselves as the latter-day equivalent of the Oracle at Delphi, to whom all matters pertaining to golf must be referred. On the other hand, it gave them an opportunity, one

9

that all Scots seize with gleeful hands, to mutter 'Sassenach conspiracy' to each other darkly and frequently.

In a commendable show of forward thinking, Mr Richardson shot off a letter to every golfing body he could think of, the R&A included, suggesting they form a gigantic committee. From St Andrews came a deafening silence. The letter had not come, they said, and one can imagine a lengthy exchange of 'It must have done, I popped it in the letterbox myself' and 'Well it did'nae come' consuming several weeks.

Still, matters had to proceed, and next on the list was how to deal with the awkward fact that Britain was seen as one country but wanted to send four teams, one each from Scotland, Ireland, Wales and England. No problems there. Each country could send four teams, and if that meant, say, Luxembourg scratching around to find enough golf balls in the country to fuel so many, what did it matter? At least the British would be able to enter their best men.

It then occurred to someone that there were likely to be so many chaps with golf clubs turning up that there was little hope of getting them all round the designated courses in the allotted time. Preposterous, came a Scottish growl carried on a northerly wind from St Andrews, and the R&A forthwith let it be known to all and sundry that these shenanigans were nothing to do with them and they didn't recognise the validity of the proceedings. Even in those early days the press had its ear to the ground and pronounced the whole farce doomed – to partial failure at the very best. By the time the summer of 1908 arrived, even Mr Richardson had to concede defeat. Only one valid entry had been received – from the current Olympic title holder, fifty-year-old George Lyon. He refused the gold medal. Since he was Olympic champion-in-residence, there was clearly little point in playing himself. Nevertheless, however posthumously, he is the Olympic champion to this day.

'The Games must be more dignified,' wrote Baron de Coubertin, 'more discreet, more in accordance with classic and artistic requirements.' Golf was accordingly struck from the list of Olympic sports, and only in very recent times has the IOC begun to consider reinstating it. It means that George Lyon will have remained Olympic gold medal holder for golf for at least a century.

Vardon Almost Sinks Without Trace

Harry Vardon sets off for the US Open, 1912

To this day no one has captured the British Open championship more times than Harry Vardon. Winner for the first time in 1896, he went on to claim six Open titles in all and, for good measure, went to the States in 1900 and won *their* Open as well. He was the supreme shot maker of his day and, if not quite the innovator of the overlapping grip, certainly its foremost advocate in establishing it as *the* way to hold the club. He also deserves more than a little credit for informing a member of the temperance movement that 'moderation is essential in all things, but never in my life have I been beaten by a teetotaller'.

Vardon's first four Open titles came in a seven-year period between 1896 and 1903, and it was beginning to look as if his most successful years were behind him when, in 1911, he won the title again on the same course where he had succeeded on the third occasion, Royal St George's. With the feeling that he was back to his best form, he made what was, but for a backhanded stroke of good fortune, the biggest mistake of his career. He booked a passage to America to re-establish his name there. It is easy to imagine the frustration and despair he felt when, shortly before it was time to sail, he fell ill. It looked as if his whole season would be lost and with it his last chance in the US.

Destiny, however, was playing games with him. The liner on which he was booked was making its maiden voyage. It was the *Titanic*. Vardon recovered, stayed at home and finished second in The Open in 1912. He floated across the Atlantic without mishap in 1913 (and 1920) and finished runner-up in the US Open (on both occasions) and in 1914 captured The Open at Prestwick to establish his great record.

There is a footnote to this tale of what might so easily not have been. In 1934, after more than a decade of American dominance, Henry Cotton recaptured the Open title for Britain at Royal St George's, the scene of two of Vardon's triumphs. On each of the two first days an old man came and sat by the green of the short third until Cotton had played through, but on the third and fourth days he was missing. At the end of the tournament Cotton shook off the well-wishers and stole away to the nearby Guilford Hotel, knocked softly on one of the doors and walked into the room. The same old man was lying in bed. Without a word, Cotton placed the trophy in his hands. He peered closely at its every detail while his frail fingers caressed every contour of the cup. Slowly the tears began to trickle down his cheeks. The man who had held the Auld Claret Jug aloft more times than any other, before or since, cradled it in his arms for the last time.

Have Clubs, Will Travel

Shawnee Invitational for Ladies, 1913

'Did you have a good round of golf, sugar?' Mr J F Meehan probably enquired of Mrs J F when he got home that evening. However much he knew of his wife's temperament on a golf course, he probably wasn't prepared for an answer along the lines of 'Just dandy, honey, apart from the short sixteenth. It took me 161. Pour yourself a drink and I'll tell you all about it.' I hope Mr J F's bourbon was a stiff one. The explanation was going to take some time and he would need it to sustain him.

Mrs Meehan, clearly a lady undaunted by adversity, was playing in the Shawnee, Pennsylvania, Invitational for Ladies. On arrival at the sixteenth she hit a tee shot so poor that it landed in the Binniekill River. Golf balls in those days did not sink like a stone, so her ball floated tauntingly down the Binniekill on its journey to the distant sea. Despite the history she subsequently made, Mrs Meehan did not explain what possessed her to reject the idea of accepting a penalty shot and playing three from the tee. Possibly she'd been having a bad day and that was her last remaining ball. Maybe she was just so darn mad she was determined not to be beat by a little round object. We shall never know.

What we do know is that she got in a boat and rowed after her ball (thankfully remembering to stow her clubs aboard or there's no telling what language she might have employed), eventually overhauling it after more than a mile. That was the easy bit. Next, she had to play the ball back to land. When you think about it, it's quite a feat. The boat must be moving at exactly the same speed as the ball, and at a distance to allow you a proper swing, so it's not surprising that she needed 39 practice shots before successfully chipping her naughty ball to dry land.

This was splendid stuff apart from two further problems. First, having already played 41, she was now almost a mile and a half from the sixteenth green; and, secondly, there was a sizeable wood covering most of that distance. What with tree trunks, tree roots, overhanging branches, rabbit holes and bramble bushes, Mrs M required a further 119 shots before she was triumphantly able to sink her putt.

I hope a portrait of her hangs to this day on the walls of the Shawnee clubhouse. If it doesn't it should. Mrs M's story has been told before, but it always leaves me wondering about two things. How did her playing partner pass the time while she was away on this epic endeavour? And were the pairs behind her waved through or did she return towards nightfall to find them stretching all the way back to the first tee?

No One Ever Remembers the Man Who Finishes 55th

The Open, Deal, 1920

Walter Hagen had firm, all-American views on the way a golf professional should live – flamboyantly. Not for him the stuffy old British attitude that believed members – who were gentlemen, dash it – belonged in the clubhouse, while the professionals were doomed to falling over each other in the pros' shop. This did not sit well at all with a man who intended to make a million bucks and spend at least three times that amount. So when, at the age of 27, he crossed the Atlantic for the first time to take part in the rebirth of The Open after World War One, he did so in style.

First, there was the matter of his wardrobe, to which he paid as much attention as a woman would to planning her Ascot outfits. Into his cabin trunks went stockpiles of silk shirts and buckskin shoes, not to mention a great many pairs of colourful socks to make a vivid impression when worn with plus fours and black and white footwear. On arrival in Britain he hired a Daimler, and in that exclusive automobile he swept up to the doors of the Royal Cinque Ports Club ready for the 1920 Open. The secretary refused him admission. Dammit, who did this colonial think he was? He was a professional, and if he must change before playing there was a perfectly good door round the back by which he could enter.

15

But Walter Hagen was prepared for just such an eventuality. Professionals did not have motorcars. Couldn't afford them for one thing; knew their place for another. Hagen's Daimler was, accordingly, parked in front of the clubhouse for the duration of the tournament and from it Hagen held court. If the secretary of the Royal Cinque Ports did not already wish Hagen to perdition, he certainly did when he realised he was in possession not just of a rather noticeable motor vehicle, but of a butler as well. Hagen proceeded to take his meals, accompanied by choice wines, on a table set up beside the Daimler, attended by his butler.

He had made his mark all right, and his turnout reinforced it – white shirt with black bow tie, black and white plus fours, black and white diamond stockings and shoes to match. Regrettably, he omitted – on this occasion – to load some sting into his tail. Had he won The Open (as he was to do in 1922 and on another three occasions thereafter) his point would have been made with all the finesse of a pile-driver. But Hagen – the person to coin the saying 'No one ever remembers the man who comes second' – finished 55th in a field of 56. Oh, well. Nice try, Walter. Still, as he said himself, it wasn't that he wanted to be a millionaire: he just wanted to *live* like one. And in that he certainly succeeded.

A Barnes-Storming Response

US Open, Skokie, 1922

Gene Sarazen was born Eugene Saraceni, an American of Italian descent. And when he arrived at Skokie, Illinois, for the 1922 US Open he was an unknown twenty-year-old. He had won one minor tournament – insufficient to project his name beyond local boundaries but enough for him to strike up a friendship with the first hero of American golf, Francis Ouimet, winner of the 1913 US Open.

At Skokie, Ouimet invited Sarazen to join him and two others, Chick Evans and Jim Barnes, for a practice round, but Barnes, the current holder of the US Open title, objected in the strongest terms. What it boiled down to was that Barnes didn't want to play with an Italian-American, there being at the time a lot of prejudice in that direction. Sarazen was used to this and outwardly kept his counsel but, as he was later to admit, he used it to fire himself up. Fired up he certainly was as he stormed round the Skokie course. He had arrived in Illinois an unknown, but he left it a national figure on America's golfing scene, setting the seal on his victory with a final round of 68, at the time the lowest-ever round to win a championship.

His performance had an interesting effect on Barnes, whose title he had taken. Suddenly, he was prepared to play with Sarazen. It would be nice to think the quality of his golf had washed away the prejudice, but it was just as likely he saw a money-making opportunity, for a winner-takes-all exhibition match was arranged. The night before the big game, Barnes suggested they split the purse, irrespective of who won, an arrangement that was not unusual at the time. Sarazen firmly declined the offer.

'I didn't want any part of it,' he said. 'I wanted to show him.'

He certainly did. Sarazen walloped Barnes 6 and 5, leaving his opponent to ponder the double whammy created by his insulting remarks at Skokie. He'd inspired Sarazen to take his Open title from him, and then he'd been humiliated by him in an exhibition match. The biter bit, you might say.

'I Can't Let You In, Mate – More Than My Job's Worth'

The Open, Royal Lytham, 1926

'You have no idea how good Bobby was,' said one of Bobby Jones's great contemporaries, Francis Ouimet. Nor, unfortunately, has anyone today. Those who remember him in his prime between 1923 and 1930 would have to be ninety or more, but he is the only man ever to have done golf's Grand Slam (in 1930 this was the US Open and Amateur Championship, and the British Open and Amateur Championship) – and that remains an unequalled feat. His relationship with the British Open got off to a bumpy start. During the third round of his first attempt on the title, at St Andrews in 1921, he had already taken 46 on the outward nine when he was bunkered on the eleventh. After several spectacular flurries of sand, some forthright curses and four attempts to get out, he tore up his card, stalked off the course and, as far as Britain was concerned, that was it for 1921.

Despite his later reputation for impeccable sportsmanship and good manners, he had, as this episode illustrates, a fiery temper in his early years, and there was a suggestion that he was affected either by nerves or an inclination to take his foot off the pedal when in a leading position. It did not take him long, though, to come to grips with these flaws and eliminate them from his game.

Back home in the States, he got on the major-winning trail in 1923 with the US Open, but it was not until 1926 that he landed his first Open in

Britain. It might not have happened. He was an amateur in the days when amateurism was strictly enforced (though he was once presented with a shotgun for winning a tournament) and could afford to cross the Atlantic only as part of the American Walker Cup team, whose fares were paid. America narrowly won the Cup, but Jones, never a willing loser, had surprisingly gone down in his match. Two days before he was due to sail home he decided to stay and enter The Open to show everyone he could play a bit. The Open that year was at Royal Lytham and at the end of the third round Jones was very well placed in second position.

In those days the two final rounds were played on the same day, and at lunchtime Jones was two down to his playing partner, Al Watrous. In the break the two of them nipped over the road for some sandwiches at the Majestic Hotel, but on his return to the course Jones found, after some frantic scrabbling in his pockets, that he'd left his pass behind. By now he had a fame and reputation comparable to that of Tiger Woods today. Can you imagine Tiger arriving without his pass on the morning of the final round? 'Morning. 'Fraid I've left my badge behind, but you know me. I'm Tiger.' Would he get the answer 'Yes, mate, and I'm Winnie-the-Pooh. Hop it?' Probably not (though I wouldn't risk money on it). But that roughly equates to Bobby Jones's experience with the immovable stalwart guarding the front door at Royal Lytham.

Nothing would persuade him to let Jones in. Well, I mean, mate, anybody could say they was called Jones, couldn't they? Eventually, Bobby gave up, went round to the paying public's entrance and bought a ticket for 2s. 6d. (12.5 pence) so he could be reunited with his clubs. He duly won The Open, and came back to win it again in 1927, 1929 and 1930 before retiring with his Grand Slam.

Archie's Hopes Rise and Fall

The Open, Royal St George's, 1928

Once the Americans had tasted the pleasure of carrying off the Auld Claret Jug in 1921 (even though in that year the winner was almost more Scottish than American) there was no stopping them. Throughout the 1920s they tumbled over by the boatload to whack the living daylights out of the home-grown contestants. After his dazzling but unsuccessful (in golfing terms) expedition of 1920 (see page 15), Walter Hagen won the British Open four times, and Bobby Jones three, generally leaving one of their own countrymen to take second place, be it Gene Sarazen, Al Watrous or whoever. Only as the depression bit deep in the 1930s did the locals get relief from the transatlantic onslaught, albeit short-lived.

There was one man, though, who seemed capable of holding them and he was Archie Compston, who gave notice of his fighting qualities by finishing a single stroke behind the winner, Jim Barnes, in the 1925 Open at Prestwick. Three years later he was enjoying a good summer and threatened once again to put in a strong challenge for the Open title at Royal St George's. An exhibition match was agreed between him and Walter Hagen at Moor Park, to be contested over four rounds. In the event only three and a tiny bit were required as Archie powered home eighteen up with seventeen to play, and the British were cock-a-hoop. This, surely, was to be Archie's year.

Although the press was a shade more constrained then than it is today, it had the same tendency to build spectacular castles in the air on a single shred of evidence. What nobody bothered to ask themselves was why Walter had played so badly and whether, since he had only just walked down the gangplank from his transatlantic liner, it wasn't to be expected that he had yet to hit top gear – or indeed any gear.

Once he had finished trying on his new wardrobe and enjoyed a few parties, Walter went off by himself and put in some serious practice while Archie progressed towards Royal St George's as the hot favourite. Hagen won at a canter, his compatriot Gene Sarazen just about kept him in sight as he finished second, and poor old Archie trailed in third, well back. He never did win The Open, though he had one last chance in 1930. At the start of the third round he was five shots behind, but went round Hoylake in 68 to take the lead by one stroke from Bobby Jones. It was all too much for the Compston nerves. On the last day he blew up, took 82 and Jones won the title on his way to the Grand Slam and the construction of the Impregnable Quadrilateral.

Dr Stableford Fails to Profit From His Great Idea

A new system of scoring is launched, 1932

Every club golfer who's ever hacked out of the rough knows the name of Stableford. There may even be some who kneel by their beds each night and thank the good Lord for having invented the Stableford system without knowing who or what started it all.

Dr Frank Stableford played his golf at the Wallasey and Royal Liverpool clubs. He was not alone in bemoaning the way a perfectly good medal round could be arbitrarily wrecked at the fifteenth, or whatever, hole by the sudden gusting wind that could blow up from the Atlantic. But unlike his fellow golfers he was not content just to moan about it and order another Scotch and water, so he fell to giving the matter some thought. What was wanted, he reckoned, was a way of scoring that meant that if you had one nightmare hole – or even two – your entire round was not automatically ruined.

There is no record, nor is there local anecdotal evidence, that he leaped naked from his bath and ran through the streets of Wallasey shouting 'Eureka!' when the great idea came to him. It is a pity there is not a statue in every town by which to remember this splendid man whose simple idea has given such pleasure to so many. Everybody who reads this will know his system. Just in case you don't, you score two points for getting par according to handicap; one point for a bogey; but three for a birdie, four for an eagle and five – you should be so lucky! – for an albatross. In other words, if you finish a round with 36 Stableford points you have, on average, done the course in par according to handicap. The effect is to encourage the most middling of golfers, such as your humble correspondent, to keep on hacking because the worst you can score is nothing, and you might yet get an outrageously fortunate bounce at the next hole.

Dr Stableford's excellent invention was officially inaugurated on 16 May 1932 when the very first competition employing his scoring system teed off at Wallasey. But – and here comes the biggest clanger fate ever dropped – the great and glorious Frank Stableford was destined never to win a tournament using his invention. There's gratitude for you. The only consolation is the possibility that, at this very moment, he is playing a round with the Holy Ghost and has just scored five points on the long second at the Heavenly Belfry as his mishit second from the fairway ricocheted off an overhanging branch, was deflected onto the green from the head of a watching seraph, hit the pin and dropped straight into the hole for an albatross.

Yip-a-Dee-Doo-Dah

Horror stories, 1932–56

The yips come in many disguises. Generally, we expect to see this incurable affliction on the green, putter in hand. Of recent sufferers Bernhard Langer and Sam Torrance are the most familiar victims, instantly recognisable as they are reduced – or perhaps 'elevated' is a better word – to resting the tips of their noses on the ends of their broomstick clubs. Mercifully late in his career, the mighty Ben Hogan began to be troubled, and it's said he would slowly and deliberately smoke a cigarette down to its butt before he could bring himself to face the ordeal and bend over the ball.

The most harrowing example came on the final green of the 1956 US Open at Oak Hill, where he needed a pretty ordinary-looking putt to level with Cary Middlecoff and go into a playoff. For what seemed like an eternity he stood over the ball until spectators averted their gaze, sensing his agony. At last he stabbed at the ball and rolled it well wide. It was said he was never the same player again.

A somewhat less usual manifestation of the dread disease sometimes strikes on the tee or the fairway when a player stands waggling his club head like an enthusiastic puppy overworking its tail. However many times he begins to take the club back, he never quite reaches the point where he is sufficiently at ease to let fly. Cary Middlecoff, twice winner of the US Open, was one such. He took such an age fiddling with his stance, his clubs and his collywobbles that when he was filmed they had to edit the process to prevent the viewers from leaving for the kitchen to make a cup of coffee. When Middlecoff saw the resulting (edited) clip it convinced him his problems arose because he was hurrying his pre-shot routine and he became slower than ever.

John de Forest was another sufferer, though he stayed free of the problem while he won the British Amateur championship at Muirfield in 1932. Forest was a genuine eccentric who would, if the mood took him that way, sometimes pop up as Count John de Bendern. On the strength of his British Amateur title he received an invitation to play the Masters on Bobby Jones's newly laid-out Augusta course, and there he achieved his most memorable moment without recourse to yips or waggles. At the thirteenth – where else? – his ball was trembling on the bank just above Rae's Creek. He decided it was playable if he had one foot in the water. With due deliberation and a thoughtful look on his face, he removed his left shoe and peeled off his left sock before placing his left limb, naked to the world, firmly on the bank and immersing his fully clad right one in the creek.

'An Immortality Denied to Kings and Bishops'

English Ladies Championship, Westward Ho!, 1933

If you're going to flout convention, do it in style. Gloria Minoprio certainly did so in the second round of the English Ladies Championship – and did it, moreover, on one of England's most historic courses, the Royal North Devon at Westward Ho!. Miss Minoprio had received a bye in the first round, and was due to set off from the first tee at twelve noon precisely. There were more reporters gathered round the tee platform than you would normally expect for a mere second-round game, and this was because word had got out that the lady in question would be playing, as she always did, with only one club.

In those days the aforesaid implement rejoiced in the name 'cleek', though today we would call it, more prosaically, a 1- or 2-iron (see page 5). In case of accidents, her caddie carried, with due solemnity, a spare cleek and a spare ball or two. Naturally, the press wanted to see how well she would do, thus accoutred. The copy they were about to get proved to be more interesting than they dared to dream.

Delaying her entrance by five minutes, the splendid Miss Minoprio arrived wearing a neat navy beret, a turtle-necked sweater under a bright red jacket (which she removed and handed to her caddie while she played a shot) and navy-blue trousers!

My dear, did you see the hussy? Trousers! On a *woman*! And not *any* old trousers, but well-cut, figure-hugging ones with straps under the instep to keep them *tight*. Gloria Minoprio affected not to notice the swelling veins and bulging eyes, nor to hear the barely coherent splutterings of the gallery, and got on with the game. Her trousers were, as she explained later, so very much more efficient for playing in than a long skirt.

Fleet Street hugged itself in delight, given every reason for headlines prominently featuring the words 'sensation' and 'outrage', and every excuse for adopting a high moral tone. The Ladies Golf Union pursed its lips and issued a statement deploring 'this departure from the usual golfing costume at the Championship'. Henry Longhurst, then an apprentice on his way to being the doyen of golfing correspondents, was enchanted, however. 'She will', he wrote, 'go down in posterity with an immortality that is denied to kings and bishops, generals and statesmen. It is such little excitements as this that make life worthwhile.'

Oh, yes, the golf. For a moment there I was quite carried away. She lost her second-round match in the 1933 Championship, 5 and 3. She came back in 1934, unabashed and in trousers still, and won her first-round game 2 and 1, before going out in the second. She was still sticking to her one-club rule, and in 1935 got as far as the third round, although, alas, this was only thanks to a bye and a walkover. And so it continued through to 1938, always with the one club, and trousers in the defiant position. Good for Gloria or, as Longhurst commented on hearing she had married in 1939 and emigrated to Canada, 'Sic transit Gloria'. I hope she had a long and happy life there.

The Lord Giveth, the Lord Taketh Away

The US Open, 1934

If ever you're on holiday on Speyside and find, by chance of course, you'd forgotten to take the clubs out of the boot before you left home, drop in and play a round at Grantown-on-Spey. It's a very pleasant course, and on it Bobby Cruickshank learned his golf. In the equally pleasant bar, where you'll want to enjoy a dram afterwards, there's a framed memento of one of Bobby's slightly less heroic moments, when fate dealt him two preposterous blows on the same hole.

Cruickshank was an intrepid professional who, in the relatively early days of the circuit, played many tournaments in the States, and won the 1932 PGA Championship there. In the 1934 US Open at the Merion Club in Ardmore, Pennsylvania, Bobby was co-leader with Gene Sarazen when he came to the eleventh hole in the final round. The green was guarded by a stream, and although the distance suggested an 8-iron Bobby decided to risk a long 9-iron, aiming to get the loft he needed to hold the ball on the green just the other side of the water.

It looked as if his gamble had failed, as the ball reached its zenith and began to drop towards the stream, and Bobby was no doubt rehearsing some well-chosen Gaelic swearwords under his breath when the miracle happened. Rather than a sullen splash, he heard a pronounced ping as the ball hit a rock in the middle of the stream, and with one bound reached the heart of the green. Bobby hurled his club into the air with a cry of 'Thank you, Lord' – a very understandable and touching response.

Unfortunately he forgot, in his delight, to bear in mind the possibility that the Lord might subscribe to the chaos theory of the universe. Describing a pleasing cartwheel in the upper stratosphere, the club began its long descent to earth. Since lovers and sportsmen are trained to keep an eye at all times on the object of their passion, it was perhaps a little surprising that Bobby forgot this cardinal rule now. The lesson was painfully embedded as the club straightened like a Stuka in a dive and inflicted a direct hit on the lightly protected Cruickshank head. They eventually got him into an upright position, with or without benefit of hip flask (why does history so rarely record the really interesting details?) and he played on, despite a feeling of uncertainty about whether he was on his own legs or someone else's.

Understandably, he was five over par for the seven holes remaining, finishing two strokes behind the eventual winner, Olin Dutra. Bobby Cruickshank never did quite scale the heights, being runner-up in four different majors. On the other hand he put $100 on Bobby Jones to do the Grand Slam in 1930. Being a canny Scot, Bobby C told his friends he'd won $10,000, but the *New York Times* revealed the real amount – $108,000 – so the drinks were on Bobby after all.

Jimmy's Career Nearly Dies in Juarez

Demaret almost fails to make it to the Masters, 1935

Jimmy Demaret was as popular a golfer as there's ever been. He loved company, and other people loved to be with him. Time taken up practising golf was time wasted from a party or just a good ol' convivial get-together. 'Not only did Jimmy never practise,' growled Sam Snead. 'I don't think he ever slept.' He had other claims to fame. If you thought Walter Hagen was a snappy dresser, you should have seen Jimmy – 'the peacock of the tour' they called him on the circuit – who had a collection of shoes to rival Imelda Marcos, and thought nothing of appearing on the first tee in a glaring shirt and pants, the whole topped off by a red tam-o'-shanter. He was also pretty useful with his clubs.

He was runner-up to Ben Hogan in the 1948 US Open, but it was Augusta where Demaret really came into his own. In 1940, in a field containing Hogan, Lloyd Mangrum, Byron Nelson and Ralph Guldahl, he opened with a first-round 64 and stormed on to achieve the first of his three Masters titles, the others coming in 1947 and 1950 and making him the first to win so many green jackets. Yet he nearly blew the lot before he was even on the circuit.

He left his native Houston, in Texas, in 1935 with a car and a set of clubs to see if he could make a living playing golf. To help him through the early weeks, he had persuaded various kindly members of the community to lend him money, which, when added together, amounted to $600. He'd barely lost sight of Houston in the rear-view mirror when he came across an inviting-looking pool table in Juarez and got into a game for rather high stakes. First up, he lost the $600. Next went the car and, in a last desperate throw, he pawned his clubs and laid out the cash he got for them – and lost that too. Thankfully for a great guy, a good golfer and a spectacular dresser, he refused to gamble the pawn ticket. His brother bought his clubs back for him and he resumed his journey to stardom on foot.

When Johnny Met Harry

US Open, Baltusrol, 1936

From the perspective of the twenty-first century, it's almost impossible to imagine how loosely golf tournaments were organised half a century and more ago, and what a low profile they had with the general public. For a start, prize money was small or even nonexistent. An event in Kansas in 1932, admittedly at the height of the Depression, heaped 35,000 pounds of crushed rock salt on the unfortunate winner, who probably screamed and fled across the state boundary before they could force him to take it away. When the first Masters tournament was held at Augusta in 1934, it was not seen as a major competition, but an opportunity for Bobby Jones to gather his golfing friends together. He refused to sanction the title 'Masters' for the gathering, considering it far too pretentious.

Then there was the lack of communication while play was in progress during a major event. Out on the course you had no idea what your competitors were up to, nor, therefore, how you were doing in relation to the rest of the field. It was not that it was considered bad form to want to know, simply that the only machinery for letting you know was a friend, or fellow contestant who had finished the round and was willing to walk out and tip you the wink.

Harry Cooper was one of those golfers who, in their day, have carried the label 'greatest golfer never to win a big championship'. He had finished runner-up in the 1927 US Open, and in 1936 he was again in contention for the title, had he but known it, and was therefore giving it his all as he came round the final nine holes. He was on the fifteenth when Johnny

Bulla, who was already finished and in the clubhouse, took the trouble to walk back and pass the good news on to Harry.

'I've checked the scores,' Johnny told him excitedly. 'You can't lose. It doesn't matter what you do from here.'

As any fool knows, there is no such phrase as 'can't lose' so long as there is anyone still vertical and out on the course, but unfortunately Harry believed Johnny. Either that, or the news completely unnerved him. He immediately three-putted the fifteenth for a bogey, and racked up another at the par-three sixteenth. He rallied sufficiently to hang onto his par at the seventeenth, and then got himself onto the final green in two shots. In so far as there were crowds at big golfing events in those days, they were lightly marshalled, if at all. Such as they were, they were milling around the eighteenth green, this being the final round, and no sooner had Harry's playing partner reached the green than his pocket was picked and he took off in pursuit of the thief. It was ten minutes before he came panting back, by which time Harry had almost forgotten why he was there. He three-putted for an aggregate 284 that should have been three shots better, only to find he'd lost by two shots to Tony Manero. And that was the closest he ever got to a big title.

Play It Again, Sam

US Open, 1939 and 1947

Sam Snead was one of golf's great winners – except when it came to the US Open. Show him more or less any PGA event and the odds were that Sam would win it. He took quite a shine to the Masters as well, and somewhat reluctantly even landed The Open. Reluctantly, because Sam wasn't one to leave good ol' home comforts willingly, and if his sponsors hadn't virtually frogmarched him to St Andrews in 1946, he wouldn't have entered. As it was, he lived on baked beans for the duration and after one look at the world's most famous golf course declared it to be 'the kind of real estate you couldn't give away'.

But the US Open defeated him utterly, and one way or another he contrived to blow his chances year after year. In 1937 he was back in the clubhouse looking a certain winner only to watch helplessly as Ralph Guldahl landed an eagle to keep his title. But he was only 25 and there would be other chances. There were. In the 1939 Open at Spring Mill, he started the final round leading by one and, with two holes left, every chance that he would break seventy.

But on the eighteenth it all went terribly, horribly wrong. Byron Nelson, the eventual winner, had finished with an aggregate score of 284 and Sam needed only a par five on the 550-yard final hole to finish on 283 and take the title. Unfortunately, he didn't know that. This was long before there was a scoreboard at every turn giving players and spectators alike details of what the other contenders were up to, together with their star signs and inside-leg measurements.

Sam was under the impression he had to shoot a birdie and, being Sam, he laid back his ears and went for it. He began by hooking his tee shot into a trampled area from which the spectators had been cleared and then, still under the impression he had to make a birdie, tried to clear some bunkers between him and the green. He failed, of course, or there'd be no story to relate, and made matters worse by jamming the ball deeper into the sand with his third. Finally on the green in five, he had a 35-foot putt to tie with Nelson and at least salvage a playoff, but he missed it, took two more and finished with an eight. Goodnight, Sam. But he was only 27 and there would be other chances. There were.

In the 1947 US Open he was in a playoff over eighteen holes with Lew Worshan. They were all square on the final green and both had short putts between two and three feet. Sam's ball appeared to be a fraction further from the hole, and he was in the process of lining it up when Worshan called for the distances to be measured. This confirmed that it was Snead to putt first, so he began all over again, missed it and Worshan became the new US Open champion. But Sam was only 35 and there would be other chances. There were, but he blew them. He finished second in 1949 and again in 1953, by which time he was 41. There were no more chances.

The Early Birds Fail to Get the Worm

US Open, Canterbury, 1940

In 1940, Europe had other preoccupations than golf. Hitler was trying to carry the Channel with a long drive, and courses all over Britain were doing war service as training grounds for assaults on things other than low-scoring records. On the other side of the Atlantic, things carried on much as usual, and the annual Open was contested at Canterbury, Ohio, with the customary enthusiasm.

You would have thought that, by 1940, word would have got about that the laws of golf are many, varied, precise and punitive and that anyone choosing, or even happening accidentally, to flout them runs very considerable risks. It's rare to be bundled into the slammer, admittedly (although see page 101), but many a chap's aspirations have been ruined by the range of penalty strokes on offer for the most arcane misdemeanours, and that's just what happened to Porky Oliver in 1940.

There he was, pacing the locker room floor, with his mates, Ky Laffoon, Dutch Harrison, Johnny Bulla, Duke Gibson, old Uncle Claude Harmon and all padding up and down in line astern and glancing anxiously out of the window from time to time.

'Look's like a storm's brewing up,' said Porky (or words to that effect) to Ky, Dutch, Johnny, Duke and Claude. And indeed it did and it was. Nor was it entirely unexpected. It had been forecast, and in those pre-computer days the forecast was quite often right. Porky, Ky, Dutch etc.

picked up their clubs and legged it to the first tee to get started before the rain began tipping down.

Arrived at the tee, they found one marshal, sleepy; one scorer, unofficial; and assorted journalists who had misread the time, none of whom were expecting any activity for a further 28 minutes precisely, at which point the first tee-off time would come into effect. The marshal came to with a start and explained to the players they couldn't start for another 28 minutes. 'Nonsense!' (or words to that effect), said Porky, Ky, Dutch etc., reaching for their tee pegs. Two reporters, from the *Washington Post* and the *Washington Times Herald*, who, astonishingly, considering they were journalists, knew the rules, then joined the debate. They quoted eloquently and at length from law this, subsection that and qualifications *x*, *y* and *z*. 'Balderdash!' (or words to that effect) cried Porky, Ky, Dutch etc. in unison, and headed off down the first fairway in two groups of three.

Officialdom was outraged. You might have heard the huffing and puffing from the tenth tee, and stern words were exchanged when the six completed their round wet, but not as wet as the rest of the field, who'd set out at the times appointed.

Matters simmered quietly while play was still in progress, but when it emerged that Porky's score put him in a three-way tie for first place with Lawson Little and Gene Sarazen, the committee pounced. Porky, Ky, Dutch, Johnny, Duke, old Uncle Claude Harmon and all were summarily disqualified for teeing off out of order and seizing an unfair advantage. All but Porky wandered off with a general air of unconcern, but Porky stamped his trotter vigorously. Lawson Little and Gene Sarazen joined in on his behalf, though with what degree of enthusiasm was never recorded. But rules were rules and could not be flouted. The playoff took place without benefit of Porky's presence, and he went through life without ever winning a major.

The Putts That Wouldn't Drop

The Masters, 1946 and 1989; The Open, 1983; the US Open 1956

Missed putts in close proximity to the cup and in embarrassingly public places are as much part and parcel of the professional golf circuit as they are of the local medal round or the friendly four-ball. They are one of myriad ways in which golf builds character, however mystifying it is when God singles *you* out for reformation. Ben Hogan was blissfully unaware of the character development in store as he walked up Augusta's fairway in 1946 on his way, as he thought, to his first Masters title. He was leading Herman Keiser and had only to sink his twelve-foot putt before he could lift his hat and take the applause of the gallery. He missed. Hmm. It looked like a playoff, but what the heck! This Keiser had never come near a major and he looked like a feller who never would. He approached his second to pop it in, and missed. Hogan three-putted and Herman suddenly became just the regular sort of guy to win a major.

Forty-three years later, Scott Hoch finished the fourth round at Augusta level with a young lad from England called – hang on, I've got it here somewhere – Nick Faldo. He moved smoothly into the first hole of the playoff and reached the green in better shape than his opponent. He needed only a tiddling thirty-inch putt and the Masters was his. He missed it, and the rest is, as they say, history.

Hoch never did land the title, whereas Faldo birdied the next hole and ever thereafter made a speciality of glowering his opponents into submission (see pages 103 and 116), and accumulating three green jackets for his wardrobe.

As for poor old Hale Irwin, he produced the most televisual miss of them all in the 1983 Open at Royal Birkdale. He was twice a US Open winner so you could hardly call it nerves when he contrived to miss a putt that, if you stretched your imagination a little, might have been as much as two inches from the cup on the fourteenth green. He attempted a casual tap, bounced the putter head on the ground and over the ball. A whiff, a palpable whiff. He finished second, one shot behind Tom Watson, and that was as close as he ever came to the Open title.

He might have taken a leaf out of Henry Cotton's book. Playing with Jimmy Demaret and Cary Middlecoff in the 1956 US Open at Oak Hill, Cotton faced a tap-in of similarly daunting length to Hale Irwin's. He went to pop it in one-handed and completely missed the ball. Assuming his most nonchalant stance, and without displacing a single hair of his well-groomed head, he informed his startled partners that he had overbalanced just as he was about to play, and had merely used his club, don't you know, to steady himself. Suspecting – quite possibly with good reason – a dastardly British plot in all this, Middlecoff and Demaret sent for a ruling that, lacking any evidence other than the players' own say-so, inevitably went Cotton's way. The two Americans maintained a frosty silence for the rest of the round and refused to sign Cotton's card at the end of it, but, as Middlecoff went on to win and Cotton was seventeenth, the outcome was unaffected.

What Are Friends For?

The Open, St Andrews, 1946;
The Masters, Augusta, 1949

These days we're used to the idea of golf stars who are well paid, and superstars who are millionaires. The coming of television and sponsorship has vastly increased the number of tournaments all over the world and, given a reasonable level of talent and temperament, the rewards are considerable. It wasn't always so.

From the 1920s to the 1950s prize money, even in real terms, was small and often did little more than cover expenses. A player aimed to become well enough known through winning tournaments to draw paying crowds to exhibition matches, and to make a living that way. It followed, of course, that expenses in travelling from one venue to another were something to be kept to a minimum and, on the American circuit, golfers who got on well would often travel together and divide costs and winnings between them.

Sam Snead and Johnny Bulla were and remained good friends, and in their early days they travelled the circuit together. On Sam's very first year of tournament golf, he and Johnny clambered into one car and set off in company. As they went, Sam suggested they go 50–50 on the summer, splitting expenses and winnings down the middle. Johnny chewed this over for a bit, weighed up their respective merits as golfers in his mind and politely declined. This proved a costly mistake. That year, Sam finished in the top ten on 23 occasions, winning five events, coming second in three and third in five and, overall, was second in the US money list for the season. It would be another two years before Johnny got to finish at the top of a leader board (though such things had yet to be invented).

Having put his foot in it once, Johnny couldn't wait to do it again. World War Two had barely finished before he suggested to Sam that he should cross the Atlantic with him and have a crack at The Open in St Andrews. Being one of those Americans for whom anything beyond Uncle Sam's shores is second-rate and uninviting, Snead gracefully declined his friend's proposal, but Johnny persisted. The prize money was only £600, and the man of whom it was said 'Sam earned $1million from golf and saved $2million' could see at once that his expenses would comfortably top the winner's cheque. But Johnny persisted and so did Sam's sponsors, and in the end he agreed to go, if only to keep Johnny quiet. He won, and Johnny Bulla finished runner-up. Worse still, the only other occasion he came close to winning a major was the 1949 Masters, where he again finished second – to Snead. But, for all that, they remained lifelong pals.

Eddie Martin Puts His Foot In It

US Open, Canterbury, 1946

Byron Nelson was about as good a golfer as a good golfer ought to be. A beautiful, relentlessly accurate striker of the ball, he won both the Masters (1937 and 1942) and the US PGA (1940 and 1945) twice, and the US Open in 1939. In 1945 he won a total of eighteen tournaments, eleven of them in succession, and found it so easy that he began to get a little bored by it all. As he left for 'work' one morning, he told his wife he'd like to 'just blow up and get this over with'. When he got home she asked if he'd blown up, as desired. 'Yes,' he replied. 'I blew up and shot 66.' His ambitions were always limited to making enough to buy and run his ranch in Texas and, when he achieved that, he left the scene.

He might well have done so with a second US Open championship to put in his trophy cabinet, if he bothered with such things, but the fates took the 1946 title away from him in a fashion that would have upset a lesser man. As was the case before TV arrived to make superstars of the players and attract crowds in vast numbers to watch them play, spectator control was pretty lax. Sometimes there would be a few ropes strung on poles with the odd marshal to keep people in place, and sometimes none at all. On the credit side, those who came usually knew their golf and were generally pretty good at policing themselves but, all the same, it could get a bit congested around the greens.

In the third round, Byron played a good approach shot to the edge of the thirteenth, or sixteenth, green – and if this sounds uncertain it is because no two writers seem to agree precisely where the Dreadful Deed occurred, though we *can* be sure (I think) that it was at Canterbury Golf Club in Cleveland, Ohio.

The players had to push their way through the throng and scramble under the rope, and as Eddie Martin went to clear it Byron's heavy bag made him stumble and, according to the version you prefer, either kick or stand on the ball. The penalty stroke thus incurred may well have cost Byron victory, since he finished all square with Lloyd Mangrum and Victor Ghezzi and lost to Mangrum in the playoff. If he was upset, he didn't show it. A man who, before he played an exhibition round, would make discreet enquiries at a course to find out who held the record and, if it was the local pro or an amateur, take care not to beat it, was hardly likely to turn on poor Eddie Martin. At the end of the 1946 season he retired, at only 33 years old. As he said, he'd had enough of all the travel, parties, dinners and speeches – of being treated like a star, in fact. He was content to go home to Texas and breed pedigree cattle.

Very occasionally, he could be tempted to get his clubs out again. In 1951, after five years away from competition golf, he joined a high-quality field at Pebble Beach for the Bing Crosby Classic. Nobody stood on his ball, and he won, of course.

Go Away, You're Too Good For Us

Bobby Locke on the US circuit, 1948

Because South African Gary Player's long career coincided with the virtual start of televised golf, it has tended to eclipse the extraordinary achievements of his compatriot Bobby Locke, at least in the public mind. Locke began his career as an amateur before World War Two and when he was able to return to golf once hostilities were over, finished second behind Sam Snead in The Open. He invited Snead to play a series of exhibition matches in South Africa and, to Snead's considerable chagrin, proceeded to trounce him 12–2. No matter that Snead consistently outdrove him, the moment the pin hove into view Locke became unbeatable. His touch on the greens was uncanny. His crushing victory decided him to turn professional and he set off for the States forthwith.

On arrival there in 1947, Locke left a trail of open-mouthed pros behind him, no more able to believe the wallopings he was handing out than Snead had been. It was easy to understand their mortification. No one ever looked less like a great sportsman than Bobby Locke. Now aged thirty he was – how shall we put it? – a well-rounded figure of around fifteen stone, with drooping jowls and several chins all hidden under an unfeasibly floppy flat cap. His clothes hung around him hopefully rather than with conviction, he usually played in a collar and tie and his swing was not exactly a thing of beauty. And yet, in just a few months, he stashed away quite a few thousand dollars.

On being asked at the end of the season if he had found it difficult to adjust to American conditions, he admitted he had: 'I very nearly lost four of the first five tournaments I played there.' Not surprisingly, he was keen to return to win a few more in 1948 and, once again, emerged victorious on several occasions, in one event heading the field by sixteen strokes and thereby setting a record for the US Tour. This was too much for the Americans puffing along in his wake, so they put their heads together and came up with a pretext (that he had failed to show up for two events in which he'd been down to play) to get him banned from the circuit.

To their credit, there were many Americans who thought this an outrageous way to behave, and not surprisingly Locke thought so too. He turned his back on America and pointed himself in the direction of Britain instead, walking off with The Open in 1949, 1950, 1952 and 1957. Now aged forty, he retired from professional golf with his winnings invested for old age in a block of flats in a fashionable suburb of Johannesburg. There was no way of telling then that in the long run this would prove a bad mistake. Over the years, the nature of the suburb changed and declined. Bobby Locke died in 1987, but his wife and daughter lived on in the flats, trying and failing to sell the block as the neighbourhood decayed around it. With little to live on, they solved the problem in their own way. Locked inside one of the flats they took their own lives.

A True Sportsman – But He Lost All the Same

The Open, Sandwich, 1949

Bobby Locke's first Open win came at the expense of the unlucky Irishman Harry Bradshaw although, being the fellow he was, he never bemoaned his bad fortune. In a way it was just as well, because he could have avoided the problem with a little more patience.

The 1949 Open was played at Royal St George's in Sandwich, the first English club ever to stage the tournament back in 1894, and Harry was in the form of his life. After the opening day he led the field with a first-round 68 and his putting, the strongest part of his game, was working like clockwork. At the fifth hole in his second round, he reached his ball to find it lying among a pile of broken glass (later legend said the bottom half of a broken beer bottle, but this arose because of a later posed photograph).

The question was whether he was entitled to a free drop. He thought he was, but he could not be sure. Was the glass a loose impediment that could be moved (it certainly was), or was it a man-made obstruction that could not? Nowadays, a player would send for an official ruling, however long it took. Harry had the option but he didn't like to hold up play. He was a man with deeply held beliefs, among them the view that one did not try to bend the rules to one's own advantage.

He elected to play the ball as it lay, took out his wedge, shut his eyes and let fly. His reward was a shower of splintered glass in the face, and a ball that hopped forward an apologetic twenty yards. Harry took a double-bogey six. He was very upset by the incident and the flying glass, and his normally secure putting went to pieces, leaving him with a round of 77.

By the following day he was back to normal and his third and fourth rounds were 68 and 70 respectively, which left him tied with Bobby Locke. The playoff was over a marathon 36 holes, and Locke trounced him by twelve strokes. If only he had held firm and sent for that ruling on the second day. But he was much too cheerful a man for regrets. Years later he said, 'True, if I'd sent for a ruling I might have won the championship, but it wouldn't have been right. Locke was by far the better player and deserved to win.' There is the voice of a real sportsman.

Herman Fails to Lick the Stamp

The Open, Troon, 1950

Herman Tissies is not a name that has come down to us echoing around the cavernous hall of golfing fame. More than half a century ago he was something of a rarity, an amateur from Germany, and he decided to have a crack at The Open. If it was his intention to create a legend it was a good move, if not altogether in the way he envisaged.

Troon possesses a hole that is renowned the world over, the wee par three Postage Stamp with its tiny green and formidable array of sentinel bunkers waiting to swallow any marginally errant ball. It can make or break a round and a reputation. In 1973 Gene Sarazen, then in his seventies, played a couple of exhibition rounds at Troon for old time's sake. Unlike Herman Tissies 23 years earlier, he well and truly licked the Postage Stamp, taking three shots over two rounds without removing his putter from the bag. First time round, he holed in one; the second time, he hit his tee shot into one of the bunkers and holed from there. His 36-hole score in 1973 was identical to the one he had made on his last visit to Troon as a 21-year old in 1923. The American columnist, Art Spander, recalls an old member who buttonholed the great man in the clubhouse and complained: 'Fifty years, Mr Sarazen, and you haven't improved a single shot.'

Herr Tissies, on the other hand, found the going trickier in 1950. Unlike Sarazen, he did use his putter, though just the once. It wasn't so much the putting as what went before that made his day somewhat dispiriting. His drive drifted left into a bunker. With Teutonic determination, he plunged into the trap with his sand wedge and was gone some time. Eventually – to be precise, after five attempts – a ball emerged, flew across the green and disappeared into one of the bunkers opposite, that is to say on the right of the hole. Herr Tissies stalked around the green and vanished, not forgetting his sand wedge, for a second time. In all probability, the course stewards were not proficient in German or else they might have quailed at the language floating out of the sandy depths as, once again, Herman's club rose and fell five times before dispatching the ball back across the green and into the bunker to the left from which it had originally escaped. But now he was beginning to get the hang of things and after only three more attempts he emerged, red-faced no doubt but unquestionably triumphant, to sink his putt for an epic fourteen and acquire a footnote in golfing history.

Admiral Benson's Bunker

A tale of St Andrews, possibly the 1950s

Halfway down the left-hand side of the twelfth fairway of the Old Course at St Andrews is buried a pot bunker of almost perfect dimensions for accommodating the human body. From the tee it is virtually invisible and more than one woefully inadequate golfer, myself included, has hooked a tee shot either into it, or too close to it for comfort.

After marvelling once more at the astonishing way in which this, and for that matter many another, bunker has the ability to jump into the path of our ball, we have sometimes passed judgement on its parentage and enquired after its name. This particular one, it seems, is known as Admiral Benson's bunker and your informant, if local and a devotee of the Old Course, will wait for you to ask why with barely concealed impatience. It has to be said that the degree of embroidery the resultant story is given tends to vary according to the time of day, the quantity of refreshment already consumed or, more likely, the urgent longing for a snifter or two once you've been shepherded off the eighteenth green.

I hope the bunker has not been filled in and erased from folklore, though it is possible the grey blanket of political correctness has done for it as it nearly did for the admiral many years ago. As it was, he dropped a clanger that provided vast entertainment to a limited audience at the time, but in today's less joyful atmosphere tends to be frowned upon by the thin-lipped guardians of PC.

As those familiar with the Old Course know, the seventh fairway runs parallel to the twelfth before veering away in a dogleg towards the green it shares with the eleventh. The admiral's seafaring days were long done, and he enjoyed nothing more than a postprandial wander round the course armed with his clubs, especially after downing the odd G&T or four. He had played his drive at the twelfth, long but wayward, and was tottering down the fairway towards it when he spied on the port bow a lone golfer coming up the seventh. Indeed he could hardly miss the figure on two counts: first, it was unmistakably a lady golfer; secondly she was most fetchingly attired in a brilliant letterbox-red outfit.

'Ah-ha!' (or possibly 'Ahoy!') cried the admiral, raising a quavering arm in her general, but unsuspecting, direction. 'Wouldn't mind posting a letter there, what.'

With which disgraceful but, to him, happy thought he toppled into the aforesaid pot bunker, which fitted him like a glove, and fell soundly and stertorously asleep. All efforts to wake him proved unavailing. Since it would clearly be deuced bad form to leave him in the bunker, tempting later wayward drives to bounce off him back onto the fairway, help was summoned from the clubhouse, to which he was returned on a makeshift stretcher. The tale, needless to say, had done the rounds of the august R&A before he had awoken to order another G&T.

The Right Direction to Hurl a Club

Golf can bring out the worst in you, 1950s

It's an infuriating game. How do you react when you make a mess of the perfect shot you knew you were about to strike? If you're one of those very lucky, very calm people, you banish it from your mind and concentrate on nothing but getting the next one right, the golfing equivalent to cricket's Mike Atherton and Herbert Sutcliffe, who could instantly forget the previous ball that had so nearly dismissed them. If you're the other sort, finding release by hurling your clubs all over the fairway, you're in good company. There have been some eminent golfers with fuses of remarkable brevity. Once the blue touchpaper was lit there was no time for escape.

Lefty Stackhouse, a between-the-wars player, practised a compelling line in self-abuse when he felt he was to blame for things that were less than perfect or, if it was clearly the club's fault rather than his own, he would see to it that the club never played again. From time to time he would wreak vengeance on the entire bagful of clubs for exerting a bad influence on the one that had offended him. On one occasion his caddie became implicated in the error of the day, and he followed the bag and the clubs into the nearest lake.

Lefty's mantle passed first to Ivan 'the Terrible' Gantz and later to Terrible Tommy Bolt or, as he was inevitably known, Thunder Bolt. In the 1940s, Gantz was liable to beat himself in the face with the club that had just betrayed his talent or, if he felt he was being too lenient with himself, grab the nearest rock and repeat the dosage. Now and again he was to be found inflicting severe damage on oak trees with his head. On many an occasion he would terrify spectators by rolling around the fairway, biting the grass in rage or, if it was a bunker that had set off the chain reaction, eating mouthfuls of sand.

Thunder Bolt was in a different category. Not only was he a better player, winning the US Open from Gary Player in 1958, but he was less of a self-abuser, more of a club-chastiser. He always insisted that he was a pussycat compared with Ivan the Terrible, but he got the greater publicity, being more in the thick of the big tournaments. In the same round of the 1953 Tournament of Champions in Las Vegas he broke both his putter and his driver, leaving himself rather limited options for the rest of the day.

The favourite Thunder Bolt story was of the tournament in which, having arrived at the last, par-three, 120-yard hole, his caddie handed him a 3-iron. Tommy was less than impressed with his caddie. 'It's the only club left in the bag,' said the caddie, or so the tale goes. 'You've broken the rest.'

By 1957 the PGA had had enough of low-flying clubs and enacted the so-called 'Tommy Bolt Rule', penalising any player who hurled a club. No doubt it did much for standards of decorum and sobriety on a golf course, but it was water off a duck's back to Thunder Bolt. Tommy came to the eighteenth tee in an early round of the 1960 US Open at Cherry Hills and hooked his drive into a pond. He put down another ball and hooked it into exactly the same place, whereupon he hurled his driver in as well, so that it could see what a mess it had made of things. Tommy was all innocence. 'Hell, I was just taking a practice swing and the little beauty just sailed out over the water,' he said. But he got his comeuppance, because he professed to be fond of that club. A small boy dived in to rescue it, but, as Tommy went forward to press thanks and a note into his hand, the boy took off, driver and all, and neither was ever seen again.

Quite apart from his 1958 Open win, Tommy contributed one thing of note to the golfing world. He taught Arnold Palmer in which direction to throw a club, should ever the need arise. 'He was so innocent he'd toss it backwards. I had to explain that you got worn out walking back to pick it up. You have to throw your clubs in front of you if you're going to be a professional.'

Quite. Thanks, Tommy.

The Babe Hands Out a Beating

Leonard Crawley encounters Babe Zaharias, 1951

Bobby Jones reckoned Joyce Wethered, British Ladies Champion four times in the 1920s, was the best golfer, male or female, he had ever encountered, and that should have been warning enough to men that this was one of those sports that could easily produce parity between the sexes. So no patronising remarks if you please. Mind you, after Joyce Wethered there was a pause before professional women's golf really took off and it was only in the years after World War Two that it began to attract significant interest, thanks to the Americans. So perhaps there was some excuse for Leonard Crawley's not quite appreciating that he might have bitten off more than he could chew.

The American Mildred Didrikson was an extraordinarily versatile athlete. She took gold medals in setting world records for the 80-metre hurdles and the javelin in the 1932 Olympics, where she also came second in the high jump. She was a basketball international, and a baseball player who hit five home runs – and then discovered golf. She could smack an insignificant thing like a little white ball as far as anyone, but surely there was more to the darned game than distance. And it was Joyce Wethered who taught her just how much more.

The trouble, according to the arcane rules of the day, was that, since she had made money from other sports, she wasn't allowed to play golf as an amateur, and, since there were not (yet) any women professionals, she consoled herself by marrying a wrestler. He was called George Zaharias and, with a flash of inspiration, she became – hey presto! – someone else.

Colourful at the best of times, Mildred now became Babe Zaharias, registered as an amateur, and set about beating the socks off everybody else. And a comprehensive job she made of it, winning more or less everything in sight, including the 1947 US Amateur Championship and the British Ladies Open Championship. At which point American women began a professional circuit and Babe, who liked the idea of winning a few spare dollars, immediately turned pro and won roughly half of all the tournaments in which she appeared.

By the time she encountered Leonard Crawley, the Ladies Professional Golf Association had been going for some years, and Crawley for a great many more years than that. In 1951 the US national women's team crossed the Atlantic to play a team of British amateurs, among them Mr Crawley, a fine golfer and former champion (who was also a distinguished and long-serving golf journalist) and this was the cue for his clanger. Mustering all the old-world chivalry that was still a number of years from being declared null and void, and no doubt raising his hat to boot, Mr Crawley addressed Mildred/Babe along the general lines of 'You will of course be using the forward ladies tees, madam?' In reply he received an answer that, when divested of its colourful outer wrapping, amounted to 'Ladies tee, my ass!' which, God bless my soul, appeared to be a negative.

This was not the best of starts and by the time they reached the eighteenth, it had become significantly worse. Mr Crawley tottered thankfully through the door of the (men-only) nineteenth, having been, as Muhammad Ali might say, 'whupped'.

Mildred/Babe, alas, was not long to enjoy her status as one of the big three American women golfers. Barely five years later she died of cancer, still only 42, though not before she had risen from her sickbed in 1954 to win the US Women's Open one last time.

The Clown's Party Piece

The Open, Royal Portrush, 1951

In the years of austerity following World War Two, the British Open lost its standing in the eyes of many of America's leading professionals, and it was not until Arnold Palmer was persuaded across the Atlantic in 1960 and fell in love with links golf that the annual transatlantic invasion began again. Apart from one-off winning forays by Snead in 1946 and Hogan in 1953, the Open title circulated among British, South African and Australian players, with Bobby Locke (four wins) and Peter Thomson (five) the most persistent. One exception to the rule was Frank Stranahan, an American amateur who was good enough to finish runner-up in the 1947 Masters, and who was twice second in The Open, in 1947 and 1953.

In 1951, The Open went across the Irish Sea to Portrush, eagerly followed not only by Stranahan but also by the colourful Englishman, Max Faulkner, who hid his considerable golfing prowess beneath a mask of clowning and eccentricity. Faulkner eschewed the drab fashions of the bleak postwar years and followed in the footsteps of men such as Walter Hagen and Jimmy Demaret in making himself the peacock of the fairways with his colourful sweaters, plus twos and long stockings. He was obsessed with his play on the greens and made all his putters – more than three hundred of them – himself. On the eve of the Portrush Open, Faulkner had a feeling this was to be his year. His long game was in disarray, but the nearer he got to the pin, the hotter the streak he was enjoying.

His opening round of 71 was a disappointment to him, leaving him three shots behind the leaders, but on the second day he shot 70 to edge himself in front. It was as he left the dining-room of his hotel that night, that Frank Stranahan let slip a comment that Faulkner overheard and took great exception to. Stranahan was eight shots adrift of Faulkner and remarked to a fellow player that, given that it was Faulkner out in front, eight strokes ought not to be too great a problem.

Max instantly became Mad Max. Knowing he was paired with Stranahan next day, he went up to him and told him he was not so much as to open his mouth out on the course. After a good night's sleep he repented of his anger and on the tee, approached Stranahan with outstretched hand and an apology, but was met with a view of Stranahan's rigid back. In much the same way that Nick Faldo responded to Ray Floyd 36 years later (see page 106), Faulkner determined to let his clubs do the talking.

His long game fell back into place and at the sixteenth he played one of golf's great shots. He pulled his drive badly, the ball ending a foot or two inside the post of an out-of-bounds fence. It left him with an awkward choice: either (a) a wedge shot back to safety on the fairway and an outside chance of getting away with par or, more likely, a bogey; or (b) an almighty gamble that, if it came off, might make him unbeatable. With Stranahan looking on, he thrust the wedge back in the bag and pulled out his 3-wood. There was only one stance that would allow him a full swing, and that would force him to play the ball away over the fence, hoping to curl it back in again. If he failed, he would kiss the Claret Jug goodbye, perhaps for ever.

In dead silence, he struck the ball. The following gallery craned its collective neck to follow its flight. As it reached its zenith it seemed to straighten and then, slowly, to curl inward as the crowd began to shout, urging it in over the fence. As the cheering swelled to resemble a Wembley roar, the ball hit the fairway and ran on and up to the green. Faulkner looked over at the man whose attitude had been the inspiration for the shot. Unlike the Floyd–Faldo spat of later years, no grudges were being kept warm here. Stranahan was applauding Max with an enthusiasm that matched the crowd's. 'That', he said, 'is the greatest shot I've ever seen.'

In those days, both the final rounds were played on the same day. As Max made his way to the first tee for the fourth and last round, a boy thrust an autograph book into his hands. In it he wrote, 'Max Faulkner, 1951 Open Champion.' It would be eighteen long years before there was another British winner of The Open.

Miss DeMoss Takes Pity on the Brits

The Curtis Cup, Muirfield, 1952

'Women are unfit to play golf,' wheezed Horace Hutchinson, one of the leading amateur players in Victorian days – unfit for turning anything into a successfully organised venture, always quarrelling with each other and incapable of playing two rounds a day. Perhaps old Horace was playing a devious game, fully realising that nothing could be better calculated to stimulate an outbreak of women's golf, but somehow I doubt it. They tended to have strong convictions in his day, and to state them without room for alternative interpretations. Inevitably, therefore, women were playing golf all over the place in no time at all, and among the leading activists in America were the Curtis sisters, Margaret and Harriot, after whom was named the cup that was inaugurated in 1932 for the winners of matches between American and British and Irish amateur women.

The only fly in the ointment was that, as with the Ryder and Walker Cups for the men, America would keep on winning the darned thing. Twenty years after the first encounter, Britain and Ireland still hadn't got their hands on the Cup but, as Elizabeth Price (B&I) teed off with Grace DeMoss (USA) in the final pairing at Muirfield in 1952, matters were on level terms at four matches each. Hope still flickered, if not brightly. DeMoss was a tough competitor and she was in sparkling form. It seemed clear that if Price was to win she would have to play above herself all the way to the last green.

They reached the fourteenth all square and DeMoss hit a beauty off the tee, right down the middle of the fairway. Price, in answer, put her shot in a bunker. Then, without any warning at all, DeMoss went to pieces. Every shot she attempted went off the bottom of the shaft. She took six to scramble down at the fourteenth, which Price won comfortably. It was the same at the fifteenth and the sixteenth, where the game came to an abrupt and anticlimactic end in a win for Elizabeth Price. For the very first time, courtesy of Grace DeMoss's inexplicable transformation from tigress to kitten in the space of a single shot, Great Britain and Ireland were Curtis Cup holders.

Billy Joe's Doppelgänger?

The Masters, Augusta, 1954 and 1984

The elements play strange tricks, the mind even stranger ones. In the 1954 Masters, a well-known amateur, Billy Joe Patton, was leading the field through the final round, convincingly defending his one-shot lead as he kept at bay the mighty Ben Hogan, defending champion, and Sam Snead, both of them two-time winners at Augusta. Billy Joe came to the par-five thirteenth, then as now a hole that tempts the unwary to land their second shot on the green. Get it even marginally wrong – and many do – and your ball is liable to finish in Rae's Creek as it wraps its watery arm around the target. Once you've saved your ball from drowning, the next problem is to get enough undercut – by now on your fourth shot – to hold it on the green.

This was the problem confronting Billy Joe as he pondered his second. He decided he could carry the creek with a 4-wood but, even as he launched his shot, a sudden gust of wind blew through the trees and swept the ball down into the water. He couldn't get enough bite on his next shot and finished with a double-bogey seven. He finished the round one behind Snead and Hogan, and Sam Snead won the playoff.

Thirty years later, the amiable Ben Crenshaw found himself in the same spot and the same position, but this time it was Tom Watson on his heels. Ben loves everything to do with golf – its settings, its characters and its history, and probably knows as much as any person alive about the past of this great game. As he stood over his second shot he looked towards the gallery gathered alongside the thirteenth fairway, and who should he spot but Billy Joe Patton.

At once his mind flashed back to the 1954 Masters and the fate that had befallen Billy Joe at this very spot. He changed his club, laid up well short of Rae's Creek and carried on to win by two strokes and claim the first of his two green jackets. It meant a lot to him because, of all the tournaments, the Masters is his favourite. As for Billy Joe? He was certainly present at Augusta but not among the onlookers at the thirteenth. He was emphatic he hadn't been near the thirteenth at any time that day.

Picking the Right Club's the Easy Bit

The Open, St Andrews, 1960 and 1990

There are some who have won more big titles, and some who have won more money. There may be one or two who play golf today as excitingly as Arnold Palmer played it in the late 1950s and early 1960s. There is nobody who inspired more affection wherever he played, as his emotional reception in his final Masters round in 2004 demonstrated.

Nowhere is that affection stronger than in Britain. It wasn't just that he came and played in the 1960 Open and, by loving it, persuaded his American contemporaries to join him thereafter, as they did in ever-increasing numbers. Many Britons weren't even thinking in such terms. What the knowledgeable British golf fans responded to was his exciting, go-for-broke golf, the skill with which he played it, and the emotions that were never hidden. His face was an open book. It could register disappointment, anger or frustration like anybody else's, but mostly it seemed to register cheerfulness and good humour as he enjoyed himself. British onlookers responded to him, and he to them, and a long love affair was born.

He played well in 1960. He so nearly won The Open at his first attempt, finishing second to the Australian Kel Nagle, and his failure to pin it down came at the Road Hole, the infamous seventeenth that did for Tom Watson almost a quarter of a century later (see page 97). In each of the first three rounds, Palmer asked his long-serving caddie and friend, Tip Anderson, what club he recommended for the all-important second to the green. Each time, Tip told him it was a 5-iron, Arnie disagreed and wanted to use a 6, they argued about it, and Arnie ended up taking the 5-iron.

On each of the first three days he played his second shot beautifully onto the green with the 5-iron, only to ruin his chances by three-putting for bogeys. On the final day, they gathered in the middle of the seventeenth fairway and began the customary squabble about which club to use. This time Arnie resolved it by saying he was taking the 6-iron he'd been trying to use all week. He flew it straight over the green and into the road behind, the nightmare every golfer tries to avoid. But – the twist in the story – he played a magical recovery from the road, up onto the elevated green, and holed his putt. He had made his only par of the week after his worst second shot of the week with the wrong club.

'There you are, Tip,' grinned Arnie, slapping him on the back, 'you've been giving me the wrong club all week and it's cost us the championship!'

Palmer and Anderson remained a devoted pairing. Thirty years later, in 1990, Arnie came back to play The Open for the last time. Now 61 years old, he wanted his farewell to Britain to be at his best-loved course, St Andrews, and the fans bade him a rapturous farewell. For most of the second day it seemed as if he would make the cut and remain to play on through the weekend, as he longed to do, but to everyone's intense disappointment, he missed it by a single stroke. That night, he and some friends were in one of the St Andrews bars, and Tip Anderson was with them, inconsolable. He felt he was to blame for not guiding Arnie round the course better and taking that one vital shot fewer. 'I should have done better,' he said, the tears flowing. Arnie took Tip's hand in both of his and simply said, 'No, *we* should have done better, old friend.'

Playing into His Hands

Augusta Masters 1961; US Open, 1965

Never for a moment let it be doubted that Gary Player was an outstanding golfer. Starting with an unpromising body and an unattractive style, he turned himself into one of the all-time greats by dedication to fitness and practice, endless practice. The result of his dedication was nine majors, one more even than that of his extraordinary contemporary, Arnie Palmer. Even so, the number of times his opponent gave him a helping hand is remarkable.

Player's first US major came at Augusta in 1961. Palmer was then at the zenith of his career, the current US Open champion and the incumbent wearer of the green jacket, having won the Masters for the second time the year before. As he stepped onto the eighteenth tee for the fourth and final time in the 1961 tournament he needed only a par four to win outright for the fourth time or, in a worst-case scenario, a bogey five to go into a playoff with Player.

The eighteenth was shorter and less tree-girt in the 1960s than it is today and, as Arnie's drive was respectable and safe, there seemed little prospect of anything worse than a safe par. Instead, he walloped it into the bunker guarding the right-hand side of the green. The odds shifted slightly towards a bogey five but, when the third short climbed above the green and came to rest in the crowd around it, Gary Player suddenly began checking his card all over again. He had every right to do so, because Arnie had to chip his ball back to the green (four shots gone) missed his putt (five) and finally got the little blighter in in six. Game set and green jacket to Player.

It was thirteen years before he won again at Augusta, and then he did it in both 1974 and 1978. Once more he had a helping hand, this time from Hubert Green, as good a putter as you could wish to find. Green needed a putt of marginally over three feet to tie with Player and yet, maybe with thoughts of Doug Sanders's plight at St Andrews in 1970 (see page 80), couldn't quite bring himself to believe he could do it. He got up, backed away from the putt, tried again – and missed.

Gary Player managed to win the US Open only once, and for that we have to step back to 1965, when he was involved in a head-to-head playoff with the Australian Kel Nagle. Nagle was a good, reliable golfer, rarely exciting to watch but, like a terrier, he never let go. If he had his teeth in your trouser leg, you were lucky to get away from him. Arnie Palmer had tried and failed in the (British) Open in 1960.

But Nagle had a sensitive side. I'll repeat that, because it's not often you can say it about an Australian. Nagle, as I was saying, had a sensitive side to him, and, when he pulled a tee shot straight into the onlookers and scored a bull's-eye on a dainty female head, he was excessively put out. As was understandable, since, as tends to happen when a bony part of the anatomy takes a direct hit, blood was not in short supply. Luckily, the injury proved superficial, but it shot Nagle to pieces. Whether he couldn't stand the sight of blood, or whether he suddenly felt vulnerable in a land ruled by lawyers, his game never recovered, and Player had his Open title.

A Lesson in Humility

US Open, Congressional, 1964

Ken Venturi's victory in the 1964 US Open was a deeply emotional affair with a curious link back to the first big name of American golf, Francis Ouimet. In 1913, the twenty-year-old amateur and rank outsider Ouimet had put his name down for the Open because it was being played at his local club, Brookline, Massachusetts. He won and achieved instant fame, not least because he beat two great English professionals, Harry Vardon and Ted Ray, in a playoff.

In the earlier rounds a boy of ten, Eddie Lowery, had carried Ouimet's clubs for him but, for the playoff, many thought it would be more dignified to take someone more august, at least in appearance.

'I looked at Eddie, his eyes filled, and I think he was fearful I would turn him down,' Ouimet explained later, 'but I did not have the heart to take the clubs away from him.'

Nothing could better sum up Ouimet, a man of grace and generosity. After his victory, one of the Brookline members said, 'Well, Francis, I suppose this means you'll be too busy now to play with any of us.'

'No, sir,' Ouimet replied. 'Shall we make a time for next Tuesday?'

Eddie Lowery grew up to be a successful businessman on the West Coast of America, but he retained a close interest in golf, and he never forgot the lessons of thoughtfulness and humility that he'd learned from Ouimet. He numbered among his own friends Byron Nelson (see page 43), and he much admired the play of a dashing young amateur called Ken Venturi who, in the early 1950s, was attracting a great deal of attention.

He wanted to help him, and to put him in touch with Nelson to develop his talent, but on getting to know him thought he detected in him an arrogance that would work against future success, and would certainly not recommend him to Byron Nelson. He asked him one day if he had a dictionary at home, and told him to 'go and look up the meaning of the word "humility", because you don't have any of it'.

You might not, strictly speaking, call a character defect a clanger. I prefer to see it as an error that, without correction, might have cost him dear. Venturi took the point to heart, and was to be sorely tested in that very virtue over the coming years as he suffered one injury after another until in 1964, at the age of 33, he reached the nadir of his fortunes. He had failed, or been prevented, in his quest to win a major title and sponsors were no longer willing to give him automatic entry even to minor events. He begged a place, as a favour, in the Thunderbird Tournament, promising himself that this was his last chance. If he failed, he would quit golf for good. With a huge effort of will he managed third place, enough to qualify him for the US Open at Maryland's Congressional course.

On the eve of the start, he went alone to a church and prayed for strength and the confidence to play well, and asked for a sign. He received it in the shape of a letter from a Catholic priest that asked him to win on behalf of all people who were in despair and had no hope.

The third and fourth rounds were to be played in the morning and afternoon of the final day, and the heat stood at a lacerating 105 degrees, with similarly high humidity. Although Venturi started well, going out in thirty, by the seventeenth green he was hallucinating, and bogeys at the two last holes left him with a round of 66. He was in such a bad state that the doctor on the course told him to withdraw, warning him he could easily die if he went out in the afternoon. 'I've no place else to go,' Venturi replied, and picked up his clubs.

By the tenth, he was in the lead. By the seventeenth he was still ahead, but in a state of collapse, barely able to walk and playing purely on instinct. Joseph Dey, the USGA director, kept him company over the inward half. As they came to the eighteenth tee he said to Venturi, 'It's all downhill to the eighteenth green. Now hold your chin up, so when you come in as champion you look like one.'

As he sank the final putt, the man who had once been labelled arrogant, but who had gone away and learned humility, collapsed in tears. He retired from competitive golf to become an outstanding teacher, who thought nothing of declining large sums of money if he did not believe the intending pupil had the right attitude. I like to think the spirit of Francis Ouimet stood behind Ken Venturi as he holed his final shot of the 1964 US Open.

A Gatecrasher at the Party

US Amateur Championship, Southern Hills, 1965

Even today, when the prize money is temptingly large and the competition to lay hands on it greater than ever, golfers are – by and large – a remarkably honest lot. There are times, though, when the temptation to turn a blind eye on an accidental foible must be very great, the more so when it is not of your making. Which makes the charge Bob Dickson laid against himself in the 1965 US Amateur Championship all the more remarkable, knowing, as he did, that there could be only one verdict, that of guilty.

Bob had just finished the second hole of the second round of the championship when he noticed an unfamiliar club in his bag. The more he looked at it, the more it wasn't his. Like a gatecrasher at a party, it beamed cheerfully at him, daring him to throw it out. Throw it out he did, however, seizing it between thumb and forefinger and holding it at arm's length. What's more, he reported the break-in to the local law-enforcement body, a.k.a. the match referee, who promptly slapped a four-stroke penalty on him as the laws of the day decreed. It was later discovered that the offending implement had been put in his bag accidentally by a fellow competitor who, at the end of a spot of practice, had slung it in one of a whole stand of bags, supposing it to be his own.

This was bad enough, but Bob played on gamely and to such telling effect that by the time he left the sixteenth green of the final round he had a one stroke lead over his nearest challenger, Robert Murphy, the dire penalty notwithstanding. Sadly, he couldn't quite cling onto it, and

Murphy pipped him at the last pin to take the title. Happily, virtue did not go unrewarded in the long run. Two years later Bob Dickson captured the Amateur Championship at Broadmoor – no, not the prison (the punishment for an uninvited club wasn't *that* bad) but Broadmoor, Colorado.

An Outbreak of
Walter Mittys

Unexpected entrants for The Open, 1965, 1976 and 1990

I expect a good few of us have drifted off to sleep with the roar of the packed gallery in our heads as our thirty-foot putt to win the title, any title, twists and turns its way into the hole. Many a professional golfer – Nick Faldo and Tom Watson, to name a couple – have freely admitted that as youngsters they would practise approach shots imagining themselves to be playing for the British or US Open.

In the chill wind of dawn, reality returns to most of us as we assess the unlikely prospect of doing well in the next Stableford, but now and again there is the super-optimist for whom, given only the opportunity, the dream might become the fact. Tournament organisers are supposed to be permanently on guard against the Walter Mitty factor, but occasionally someone slips through the defences.

In 1965, Walter Danecki hopped on a plane from Milwaukee with his clubs and headed across the Atlantic with every intention of hoisting aloft the Auld Claret Jug at Royal Birkdale. The R&A failed to see him coming, and only after a couple of rounds well into three figures (to be precise an aggregate of 221) did the penny drop that the problem might be more than just a little difficulty acclimatising to links golf. Still, Mr Danecki enjoyed himself, though his explanation that he was 'only after the money' suggested an inability to assess his playing abilities realistically.

If the R&A hoped people would quickly forgive a little slip like this, they had another shock awaiting them in 1976. Maurice Flitcroft operated a crane in Barrow-in-Furness, so at least his travelling expenses in getting to the course were not too extravagant. He managed to infiltrate the qualifying round for The Open, where he proceeded to demonstrate how much of his employer's time was spent indulging ambitious fantasies in the seclusion of his crane-driver's cab.

He opened with eleven at the first hole and twelve at the second, going out in 61 before showing a marked improvement with 60 on the inward half for a total of 121. As he explained, he had been trying too hard at the start, 'but by the end I was finally putting it all together'. The R&A had a hard time keeping the press at bay, but Mr Flitcroft remained nothing if not optimistic. Aware that the powers-that-be were now on the lookout for him, he adopted a variety of cunning disguises that would have made Baldrick proud. He tried being an American and a Swiss before being encountered in wig, moustache and balaclava at the qualifying round for the 1990 Open, where he was listed as M James Jolly from France. He got no further than the second green before he was rumbled and removed from sight by officialdom. A pity because, as he said, 'I was not yet warmed up properly.'

A Wagnerian Disaster

The US Open, Olympic Country Club, San Francisco, 1966

Even in this age of grey power, you need to be nearing the slippered and pantalooned phase of life to remember the electric impact Arnie Palmer, and his acolytes Gary Player and Jack Nicklaus, had on the world of golf. TV coverage in shimmering black and white was in its infancy, and big money was still some years in the future, but the sight of Arnie on the charge excited a following unknown to golf before. That following was soon christened Arnie's Army, and if you doubted its potency and staying power you should have been at Augusta for Arnie's farewell Masters round in 2004.

Arnie never concealed his intentions. 'If I can hit it I might hole it' was his philosophy, and with such an attitude you might not know where the ball would end up, but it would more than likely be somewhere interesting. In years to come, Seve Ballesteros wore Arnie's mantle as if it had been tailored for him.

A hell-or-high-water approach could bring rich dividends, as it did at the 1960 US Open, where he was trailing by seven strokes as the final round got under way. 'I might still be in with a chance,' he remarked to a journalist friend. 'You'll need at least a 65 then,' came the reply. Arnie duly shot 65 to overhaul the luckless Mike Souchak.

But sometimes that same approach brought disaster trailing in its wake, as it did at the Olympic Country Club on the last day of the 1966 US Open. He was partnering Billy Casper for the last round, and added to his

76

starting lead of three shots at such a high rate of interest that by the turn he was seven up with nine to play. He was about to find out how Mike Souchak had felt six years earlier, although this time it was not Casper's brilliance that undid him but his own scarcely credible waywardness.

Quite what got into him it is impossible to say. Some believed he had set his sights on Ben Hogan's all-time aggregate record of 276, set in 1948, but whether he had or not the ball began to disappear every which way but straight. Given Arnie's powers of recovery, this was not in itself the end of the world, but on this occasion the belief that if he could hit the ball he could hole it proved an illusion. The recovery shots left him in more trouble than ever, and by the time he reached the eighteenth green his seven-stroke lead was gone and he had to hole a five-yard putt downhill to tie. That at least he managed, to take the match into an eighteen-hole playoff the following day, by which time, surely, he would have recovered his composure.

Sure enough, he reached the turn in 33 and led Casper by two shots. Faldo-like, Casper just continued to play steady golf, waiting to see if his partner would manage a second spectacular implosion and, Norman-like (see page 116), he did just that. Things began to unravel on the twelfth green, on which Arnie contrived to miss from four feet to lose a shot. That, as it turned out, was merely a prelude for Götterdämmerung on the seventeenth. Arnie took seven, and the US Open that had seemed a formality less than 24 hours earlier vanished on the wind. Many believed his confidence never fully recovered thereafter, and certainly he never added another major to the eight he already had.

'I Am a Stupid'

The Masters, Augusta, 1968

The easygoing Argentinian, Roberto de Vicenzo, was one of golf's most popular performers, partly for his play but especially for his good-natured approach to opponents and spectators alike. In his career he won a prodigious number of tournaments around the world but, since he never kept any particular track of them himself, no one could be quite sure of the exact number.

Like a good wine, de Vicenzo matured late, and at Hoylake in 1967 he became the oldest winner of The Open, beating Jack Nicklaus into second place at the age of 44 years and 93 days. His 45th birthday coincided with the 1968 Masters, and being in the form of his life, he was keen to celebrate it with a green jacket. But for the most heartbreaking clanger, he might have done just that.

In his final round he simply caught fire. His final birdie was on the par-four seventeenth and, although he followed this with almost his only false shot of the day to record a bogey five on the eighteenth, he had still completed an astonishing 65 to tie the lead with Bob Goalby on an aggregate 277. Or so he thought. Perhaps he was still suffering disappointment at dropping a shot at the last and failing to win outright; maybe, conversely, he was excited at the prospect of a playoff; or possibly he was simply too trusting.

Whatever the reason, he failed to check his card properly and did not notice that his playing partner had marked him down for a par instead of a birdie at the seventeenth. He was disqualified. 'What a stupid I am,' said

Roberto, and in all probability he was smiling from ear to ear even as he said it. Whatever his innermost feelings, the graciousness with which he accepted this cruel blow won him even more friends and admirers.

Scorecard clangers are among the most notorious of all but the daddy of the lot, at least numerically, happened to Kel Nagle the following year. In the second round of the Alcan Golfer of the Year tournament in Portland, Oregon, he completed a round of 70, scoring, with pleasing symmetry, 35 on the outward half and 35 on the way home. In a moment of over-exuberance, his marker failed to notice in which column he was putting the 35 for the outward nine, and entered it against hole number 9. Glowing inwardly after his excellent round, Kel scrawled something on the card later identified as his signature, and without so much as a consoling arm round the shoulders his admirable round of 70 was transformed into a duffer's effort in three figures. From lying second, he hurtled headlong to the bottom of the field as the blade of the cut swung well below his new score! The club with which he thumped the daylights out of the marker failed to get a mention in the local press.

'You Shouldn't Have Too Many Thoughts in Your Head'

The Open, St Andrews, 1970

To anyone over about fifty, Doug Sanders's missed putt on the last green in the 1970 Open at St Andrews remains etched in the memory. It cost him the championship, but there have been many dramatic last-hole misses, so why is this one particularly recalled? In part because it happened when it did, in 1970, just as interest in championship golf was reaching a new audience in Britain.

Thanks to Arnie Palmer's exciting approach to the game and his eagerness to cross the Atlantic in the 1960s to take part, enthusiasm for the British Open had swung rapidly upwards. Jack Nicklaus followed Palmer and added further glamour by winning the title in 1966, and in 1970 he was trailing Sanders by a shot as they came to the eighteenth at St Andrews. Finally, television was now providing full coverage of the event, albeit in fuzzy black and white that failed to do justice to Sanders's colourful wardrobe. If he didn't dress to kill he certainly did so to dazzle, though his contemporary, the irascible Tommy Bolt, was unimpressed.

'He looks like a jukebox with feet,' he once said with a snort.

There is a story that, as he waited to drive the eighteenth in the final round, Sanders was handed a white tee peg to use by Lee Trevino. It had belonged to Tony Lema, a winner of The Open in 1964, who died two years later in an air crash. Trevino meant it as a good-luck gesture, not knowing that Sanders was superstitious and never used white pegs, so, if the story is true, it was an unsettling start to what should have been Sanders's glory drive for the championship.

Nevertheless, he was on the green with a three-foot putt to win the Open title outright from Nicklaus. He bent over the putt, but then pulled out and started again. As the current British player Ian Poulter says, 'You shouldn't have too many thoughts in your head when you're putting. I've seen far too many players go down the technical route and before they know it, their brains are fuzzed.'

Sanders started again and trickled the ball wide. It meant a playoff with Nicklaus next day that he lost. Just as in the 1959 US PGA and the 1961 US Open, he was the runner-up, and he never did land a major. Afterwards, Sanders admitted, 'As I looked at that putt I was thinking about what I was going to do – throw the ball or club in the air and bow to the gallery. And try to be a humbler winner.'

Too many thoughts, Doug, too many thoughts.

Tony Sunk on the Lee Side

The Open, Muirfield, 1972

After nearly twenty years in the doldrums, British golf was put back on its feet by Tony Jacklin's capture of The Open at Royal Lytham in 1969 and the US Open at Hazeltine the following year. The key to his victories, especially at Lytham, was the brilliance of his play around the greens, especially when he found himself in a bunker. Time and again he would feather the ball to within a few feet of the pin and need only a single putt.

The final round of the 1972 Open at Muirfield is high on the list of memorable golfing days. Jack Nicklaus had not enjoyed the three preceding days and seemed out of the running until his final round of 66 made him the leader in the clubhouse. Meanwhile, a fight to the death was going on between Jacklin, who was playing superbly and led the field, and the flamboyant Lee Trevino, who was playing the kind of golf Jacklin had produced at Royal Lytham three years earlier. The minute he caught sight of the green, Trevino seemed to play a miracle shot to within feet of the pin irrespective of where his ball was lying – grass, sand or rough, it made no difference. The two of them were, said Peter Alliss, 'like two heavyweights trading punch for punch'.

And then came the seventeenth. Trevino's tee shot was wild and finished in a bunker from which he could only splash out. Next he smacked the ball into some uncomfortably *rough* rough, from where his fourth shot ran across the green and up a bank. While Trevino was exploring parts of the seventeenth that only weekend golfers were familiar with, Jacklin was just short of the green in two and pitched his third shot to within about fifteen feet of the flag. It looked for all the world as if he was about to pick up another shot, and that would virtually assure him the 1972 Open.

Trevino was self-taught and he had a simple answer for all those who plucked his sleeve and suggested he find a coach. 'If he can beat me, I'll listen to what he has to say,' he would reply. He loved playing on British links courses, running his ball between the bumps and through the hollows, and seemed to have an almost instinctive eye for the way it would twist and turn on the undulating turf. He never wasted time debating all the variables that might or might not come into play. Maybe with his eye for terrain he didn't need to.

Now he stepped up to his ball and played it – not quite as fast as later legend insists, but quickly all the same – down the bank, across the green and straight into the hole. Down in five. A brilliant recovery from adversity! If Lee had whooped and hollered before, he was demented in his delight now, and Lee's celebrations were so infectious he had the gallery in uproar too.

But, to return to sanity and the cold light of reality, Jacklin had only to putt out for a four and his lead was virtually unassailable. If he was inwardly gripped by nerves, it didn't show, but his putt rolled past the pin nevertheless. Still, if he holed the return, he would still be one up with one to play. But he didn't. It took him three putts to get down for a six, and suddenly the lead he had held so long was gone. He dropped another stroke on the eighteenth, Trevino took the title and Nicklaus found himself in second spot, one ahead of Jacklin.

Tony never quite recovered his earlier brilliance after Muirfield. He remained a very good golfer, but not the world beater he had been for three scintillating years.

Quick, Another Brandy and Soda

English Amateur Championship, Moortown GC, 1974

'Well I mean to say, old boy, it's a bit thick when a chap can't get a bit of peace and quiet in his own bar, don't you think? Bad enough toodling up for a game to find a board saying the course is closed for a week for the English Amateur whatnot.

'I mean, a whole week kept off your own course, old boy. Fluffers and I aren't best pleased, I can tell you. Eh? What's that? Fluffers? Because he's always fluffing his bunker shots, of course. Dammit, it's obvious, isn't it? Never got out in less than four in all the years since we were at school together. What? Oh, well, all right old boy, three, then, but you only managed it that one time.

'I mean to say, there we all were, all the members, quietly enjoying a snifter or two, taking refuge in the only place left to us to get away from these johnnies swarming all over the links. Never be the same again, old boy. Take my word for it – need years to recover. Anyway, there we all were when, blow me, the door opens and in comes this cove in his bare feet – well his stockings anyway, had the decency to keep *them* on – waving a club around, 9-iron I think it was, might have been a wedge I suppose. Apparently they'd put a notice up outside reminding all these chappies spikes aren't allowed in the nineteenth. Just as well if you ask me. No telling what people'll do these days.

'I said to him, "Who the devil are you?" I said. "Haven't seen you in here before. Are you a new member?" And he said "No, sir. I'm Nigel Denham. In a spot of trouble at the last. I'll be gone in a jiffy." And he pointed at this ball behind my chair. Well, dash it, I had heard a bit of a clatter but assumed it was poor old Wedgie falling out of his chair. I mean to say, he often does just before lunch. Never knows when to stop. Excuse me a moment. Barman, same again. What? Yes, brandy and sodas, and go easy on the soda. Would you like one? Splendid, make that three, will you?

'Now, where was I? Yes, so this Denham feller makes poor old Wedgie get up and move his chair. I mean, old Wedgie could barely stand upright by now – he sometimes overdoes things before lunch, or did I say that before? Then he has a practice swing or two – Denham, that is, not Wedgie – before he notices the window's shut and, blow me, he insists on opening it. Says he doesn't want a bill for breaking the glass, and giggles a bit. If you ask me he'd already had a snifter or two from his hip flask.

'Anyway, he plays his shot off the carpet, straight out through the window and lands it next to the green. Good shot, I'll say that for him. And then Wipers pipes up and— What? Because of the way he blows his nose, I'd have thought that was obvious. Wipers pipes up and says, "But are you allowed to play this watering hole before the eighteenth?" Rather good that, what? Denham laughs, and says he hopes the R&A wouldn't object, and he'd be back as soon as he'd putted out to buy us all a drink.

'I rather liked the feller myself. But do you know, an extraordinary thing happened. Apparently one of the johnnies who were looking after the rules of this championship doo-dah got on the blower to the chaps at the R&A and do you know what they said? They said there was nothing wrong with playing a shot from the nineteenth fairway because he'd been trying to reach the eighteenth green at the time, but he'd improved his lie by opening the window. I mean to say, dash it, old boy! The blighters couldn't have given a hoot if he'd broken the window and left us all in a draught.

'They only went and slapped two penalty points on the poor chap. Rum do, we all thought. Nice young feller, though. That round he bought us must have cost him a bob or two. We always put the prices up for visitors.'

(The event, the shot, the player, the question asked him by a member and the R&A ruling are real. The rest may have wandered into the realm of fiction. Who can say so long afterwards?)

Politics Can Be a Dangerous Game

American presidential gaffes, 1970–95

It was President McKinley who started the rot by taking up golf in the 1890s. He was promptly assassinated – a warning, one would have thought, to those coming after him, but not one that was heeded for long. Ever since, and with increasing persistence as the twentieth century wound onwards, American politicians failed to suppress an urge to make fools of themselves on the course, and on a number of occasions have come close to gaining revenge for McKinley by assassinating random members of their electorate.

Taft and Harding were pretty enthusiastic about the game, but it was Dwight D Eisenhower whose enthusiasm became public property. Ike, as he was known, was good enough to avoid reaching the green via people's heads, but frequently collided with a pine tree on the seventeenth fairway whenever he played at Augusta in the 1950s. Each time he came, the tree was that little bit bigger and, like a magnet, his ball homed in on it just about every time he drove the wretched seventeenth. He begged the Augusta fathers to cut it down, but they were having none of it, not even for the president of the US of A and there, to this day, it stands, waiting for Peter Alliss to tell the tale for viewers back home.

It was the 1970s that unleashed presidential, vice-presidential and senatorial mayhem on America's courses. Senator Barry Goldwater, a candidate for the republican nomination in 1964, set the ball rolling, or rather the head spinning, when he walloped an unfortunate standing thirty yards from the tee in a Phoenix Open Pro-Am. Seeing that this was his home state of Arizona, one might have expected the senator to show a modicum of concern but, with a far-right reputation to uphold, he merely snapped, 'The guy was standing too close to the ball,' and buggied off down the fairway. It tended to prove the wisdom of H L Mencken's injunction, 'If I had my way anyone guilty of golf would be denied all offices of trust under these United States.'

Inspired by Senator Goldwater, Richard (Tricky Dickie) Nixon's vice-president Spiro Agnew, one of America's dodgier V-Ps, dragged his clubs out from under the stairs and headed for the nearest course. In 1970 he started as he meant to continue by mowing down Doug Sanders, who was only just recovering from missing his three-foot putt, and The Open, at St Andrews (see page 80). Sanders made the serious mistake of taking his eye off Agnew (as did many another non-golfer) and once they had brought him round he had to continue with his head bandaged like a mummy's.

His bloodlust aroused, Spiro left Tricky Dickie to run the White House in his absence and set out for the Bob Hope Desert Classic in Palm Springs. With his first two shots of the tournament he scored three (spectators, that is), and had to be forcibly restrained and, notwithstanding his status, removed from the course to ensure there was enough of a crowd left by the end of the day. It was said that Agnew's enthusiasm for this new sport was so great that he had his golf balls printed with the legend, 'You have just been hit by Spiro Agnew', and handed them out in advance. It gave him something to aim at.

If Agnew was what you might call the Hell Bunker of golfing politicians, there was still a greenside trap ahead by the name of Gerald Ford, who succeeded Tricky Dickie as president. Ford had been, in his younger days, quite an accomplished sportsman but, to the joy of photographers everywhere, became famously and photogenically accident-prone as he grew older. Once he had finished being president in 1976, he found more and more time for golf, and first-aid posts around the country were on more or less permanent alert.

'Gerald Ford is a hit man for the PGA,' Bob Hope announced. He carved his way happily through Pro-Ams and charity classics, and was still at it in 1995, when his eye alighted on the tempting nose of a 71-year-old woman. He took aim and fired. She needed ten stitches. Bob Hope was organising the event, the Chrysler Classic, and naturally had the last word: 'Gerald Ford doesn't need to keep his score: he just counts the wounded.'

Seve Avoids a Parking Fine

The Open, Royal Lytham, 1979

You have only to say the name Seve Ballesteros to a British golf fan and you get two reactions: a broad smile and a shake of the head recalling Seve's monstrous mishits to all parts of the course.

The smile is understandable. Seve plays with his heart on his sleeve, and golf fans, British ones at least, love that as much as they admire his extraordinary shot making from seemingly impossible positions. Ask them to pick the outrageous shot they best remember and the chances are they will say 'Lytham '79, the car park'. At the time, the 22 year-old Ballesteros was battling for his first Open. He had won some good tournaments but not yet a major, and his mentor, the well-loved Roberto de Vicenzo (see page 78), had sent him on his way at Royal Lytham with the words, 'You've got the hands. Now play with your heart.' With three holes of the final round left, it seemed Seve had put a little too much heart into his drive at the sixteenth. To the world at large it looked and felt like a horrible mistake that was likely to cost him the title. But was it?

Royal Lytham has plenty of rough, plenty of bunkers (one for each day of the year) and many holes with areas no self-respecting golfer would wish to be seen dead in. It's not so much a question of whether your shot *looks* good, but of the hazards you are keeping away from and the angle from which you play into the green. Seve knew this very well, and in practice before the tournament he was hitting his tee shots all over the place, often, if not always, deliberately, and exploring the bad places as thoroughly as the good ones.

Classic Golf Clangers

The weather was atrocious, so bitterly cold that Lee Trevino had his pyjamas on as extra protection, and the wind was forever rising and falling, changing the complexion of the course from one day to the next. Of the forty rounds played by the top ten finishers only seven were below 70, and best of them all was Seve's 65 on the second day. Nevertheless, as the final round began, life was very congested at the top of the leader board. Hale Irwin was two shots clear of Ballesteros, with five others tucked in just behind, Jack Nicklaus and Ben Crenshaw among them. In other words, it was going to be a tight finish with little room for error.

The thirteenth is a killer hole, and on the last day the wind was at its fiercest. Seve's caddie, Dave Musgrove, remembers being astounded when he said, 'We'll go for it today.' Of all days, and in such conditions. But go for it he did, and came away with a birdie three. By the time he reached the sixteenth, news had reached him that Crenshaw, his closest challenger with Irwin having faded, had double-bogeyed the hole ahead. Seve was in sight of the prize provided he stayed out of trouble. You might as well ask a dog not to bury a bone.

Between the sixteenth fairway and the one that runs parallel to its right is a tractor track that is used as a car park for major events. Seve's booming drive soared way out right into the middle of the cars, provoking white faces among the spectators and hysteria in the commentary box.

'Where is the ball?' asked Seve.

'Under the car somewhere,' replied Dave Musgrove.

Consultations ensued, an appropriate place to drop was agreed, and Seve pitched seventy yards to the heart of the green before holing a putt of between fifteen and twenty feet for a three. 'Outrageous,' spluttered his supporters, hugging themselves in glee as he took a three-stroke lead that he held to the end of the round.

So was born the legend of the wayward genius who couldn't help striking his long shots to all parts of the universe, but who always found the wizardry to recover from them. Musgrove, however, insists to this day that Seve always knew exactly what he was doing. Had he hit straight down the fairway, he would have been unable to stop his ball on the green, given the pin position. If he had gone out to the left, he would have had the howling wind behind him, but on the right he could play into it and hold up his approach shot. As the shot clattered in among the cars it looked like a championship-blowing howler. In all probability, it was really a stroke of genius.

Splish, Splash, Splosh

The Masters, Augusta, 1980

If God had meant golf courses to be surrounded by water he'd have put them on islands, but in this matter *Homo sapiens*, and especially *Homo sapiens americanus*, are very obstinate. There's far too much of this particular brand of liquid around. Ask Tom Weiskopf – but gently – and be sure not to mention the numbers 12 or 1980 unless you have a clear escape route.

Like Ben Crenshaw, Weiskopf was very fond of the Augusta Masters and wanted very much to win it. He had come second three times, in 1969, 1972 and 1975, and he had one major under his belt – The Open in 1973 – but the Masters just would not come his way. However, there was always next year, when, perhaps, his luck would change. In 1980 it did, but not in the direction he was hoping. Unlike Crenshaw, he saw no apparition to warn him of his thoughtless ways (see page 63).

He made a good start at Augusta in 1980, and his first round was just dandy until he came to the twelfth. As at the thirteenth, the green is guarded by Rae's Creek, but, unlike the thirteenth, the twelfth is a 155-yard, par three, so the tee shot must be precise. Weiskopf took an 8-iron, hit the green according to plan, and watched helplessly as his ball failed to bite and rolled back into the creek. This was not according to plan. Now Tom was a perfectionist. He was interested in playing good golf shots, with none of your pragmatic scrambling to get down somehow, anyhow. A wiser man might have given some thought to changing his club, hitting it higher or fuller, imparting greater backspin or whatever. Not Tom. An 8-iron it should be, so an 8-iron it would be.

He put down another ball – and watched helplessly as the ball failed to bite and rolled back into the creek. Hell and damnation! Stupid ball! He put down another, and watched helplessly etc. etc. Since Plan B did not, apparently, exist there is no telling how long this might have gone on. Mrs W, and in all probability many in the gallery, began to cry, wondering if they'd ever get home to dinner. Finally the ghost of Bobby Jones or some such shade relented and allowed him to land on the green and stay there. The final tally was thirteen strokes. Needless to say, Mr W did not win the Masters that year – nor, indeed, in any other year.

Splosh, Splash, Splish

World Matchplay Championship, Wentworth, 1980

Mention Greg Norman and Nick Faldo in the same breath and one vision comes to mind: that of Faldo psyching Norman into defeat, most notably at Augusta in 1996 (see page 116). Greg holds the unenviable record of losing playoffs in all the major championships, and seems to inspire opponents to pull off miracle shots that, ordinarily, they'd be nowhere near sinking. Happily for Norman, it wasn't always so, at least as far as Faldo is concerned.

As relative newcomers to top-flight golf in 1980, both in their mid-twenties, they met that year in the quarter-finals of the World Matchplay Championship. Faldo moved smoothly into an early lead and, with 25 holes played, in miserable, wet conditions, he was six up with eleven to play. Whether it was the rain and damp, whether Greg at last hit his straps, or whether it was a combination of both of those things, Nick's lead began to slip back and back, and by the time they came to the 36th hole he was only one up. Faced with a long dogleg par five, Greg saw that his only hope of forcing a playoff was to attack and snatch a birdie. He duly attacked, put his second shot in a bunker, recovered to face a birdie putt and missed it on the squelching green. His last chance seemed to have gone, with Faldo needing only to get down in two from eight feet.

All afternoon, as the rain teemed down, the players had been using squeegee boards on the greens to wipe the excess moisture away from the path of their putts. Faldo took his board and carefully cleared a dry – or at least less sodden – pathway to the cup. All open and above board. Craftily insuring himself against a possible miss, he also wiped the water away on the far side of the hole but – and this is where in an unthinking moment he made his horrible mistake – he swept the water *away* from the cup, flattening the grass in the same direction. Sure enough, his first putt ran past the hole by about five feet, leaving him to putt back against the grain of the grass. It stopped short, Norman had unexpectedly won the hole to level the score, and the next stop was a sudden-death playoff. Norman won it, and went on to beat Sandy Lyle in the final. Three years later the Greg and Nick show returned to Wentworth, this time in the final, and Greg won again.

The Hungry Road Hole

The Open, St Andrews, 1984

'A course architect's folly' is how the infamous seventeenth at St Andrews, the Road Hole, has been described. 'A golfer's nemesis' is what others have called it and it has decided many a tournament on the Old Course. It buried Tommy Nakajima's chances in the 1978 Open as he failed – repeatedly – to escape the clutches of the Road Bunker or, as it was afterwards christened, the 'Sands of Nakajima'.

Everything has to be just right from the moment you step onto the seventeenth tee. The drive, a long dogleg right – or straight over where the old railway sheds used to be – must land on the fairway or you're in clinging, heathery rough that catches the blade. Then ahead of you lies the elevated green looking like a miniature prehistoric fort, Maiden Castle removed to Scotland, its lower slopes guarded by a formidable bunker. Everything must be taken into account for your second shot. The lie of the ball on the upslope or downslope of the seaside turf, the strength and direction of the wind and precisely the right club for the conditions. To come up short of the green puts you in trouble, but to go over is a disaster, for there, waiting for you, is the stony track itself backed by its pitiless dry-stone wall; the hungry road that eats golfer's aspirations, as it swallowed Tom Watson's in 1984.

Seve Ballesteros loves St Andrews, and he wanted the 1984 Open very, very badly. But so did Tom Watson, who had won The Open five times between 1977 and 1983 and needed one more victory to equal Harry Vardon's record of six Open titles. At the start of the final round, Seve was playing with Bernhard Langer immediately ahead of the final pair, Ian Baker-Finch and Tom Watson, but by the time Ballesteros stepped onto the seventeenth tee the contest had become a tight, tense battle between him and Watson, both of them playing superb golf. 'Just about the most difficult hole in golf' is what Seve thought of the Road Hole, but although he never admitted to being intimidated by it he had dropped a shot there in every one of his first three rounds. In his press conference he said that if he couldn't get a par there when it mattered he'd come back on the Monday and go on playing it until he did. Luckily for him, he didn't need to. He took a 6-iron for his second shot and landed it perfectly on the green to secure a par four. As he came off the green, he told Nick de Paul, his caddie, that he reckoned he'd now secured himself a playoff with Watson.

Just one year earlier, Watson had played a wonderful 2-iron on the eighteenth at Royal Birkdale to clinch his fifth Open. Now, for his second shot on the Road Hole, he turned to the same club. It was a fatal mistake. He struck the ball beautifully, but he had overclubbed. The ball landed on the green, bounced once and sailed on into the road to rebound off the wall. To get back on the green in only one more shot was in itself a minor miracle, but, as he bent over his putter hoping to save par, there came a mighty roar from the eighteenth green. Seve had an eighteen-foot uphill putt for a birdie three, tuning from right to left.

He read it perfectly. The ball seemed to hang on the lip of the cup before, with agonising slowness, it toppled in. On the seventeenth green, Watson knew exactly what that meant. If he saved par, he too had to birdie the last to force a playoff. He putted – and missed. It was all over, and Watson never did win another Open. Nor, as it turned out, did he ever land another major to add to the eight he already had. The years of high glory ended with that 2-iron at the hungry Road Hole.

A Strange Failure in Course Management

The Masters, Augusta, 1985

Our subject today is 'course management'. (Quiet at the back, please – other people want to know about this.) Course management is a most important subject. You may regard it as another bit of the new jargon, a further example of the endless human quest to inflate the ordinary and make it sound portentous or, perhaps, just to baffle the ordinary punter. Until we knew better, you and I might have been content to call it common sense or realistic assessment or even, if we were getting a bit high-flown ourselves, limitation of overweening ambition.

But 'course management' it is these days, so just remember that, please, when next you're debating the consequences of clearing a bunker, a ditch, a hedge or even, if your hook has been especially spectacular, the clubhouse. It's not enough to breathe a sigh of relief when you get safely over the obstacle before you. It's all a question of what's on the other side and, assuming you know the answer or can find out without further detaining the two foursomes on the tee behind you, does it improve your chances of completing your round in the score you first thought of?

That, class, is course management, and if I could have your attention for a few moments more we will look at a case study of course management in action – or, in this particular example, a failure to put it into action.

Curtis Strange was approaching his golden years of 1987–90, during which he shot 62 on the Old Course at St Andrews in the Dunhill Cup, won the US Open in two consecutive years, and was twice the leading money earner on the PGA tour. In the final round of the 1985 Masters he came through the field on a dramatic charge that seemed certain to give him victory – as it would have done, but for a fatal error at the thirteenth, one of golf's most famous and testing holes.

Strange was not one of golf's mighty hitters and his drive left him over 200 yards from the green nestling behind Rae's Creek. Should he, as tournament leader, play safe and drop short of the creek to ensure a par, or should he go for broke, try to carry the water and hold it on the green? Unlike Ben Crenshaw a year earlier, he did not have a peerless knowledge of golfing history (see page 63), or else he might have paused to consider the fate of those before him who had faced a similar dilemma when standing on the spot he now occupied. He asked for his 4-wood.

Up in his box, the TV commentator immediately said, 'Curtis doesn't need a three and he can't afford a six.' The thought that should have been going through Strange's head was that he didn't need a spectacular eagle three at this hole, being in the lead with future shot-saving chances to come on later, less demanding, holes. He should also have been considering that the consequence of having an unnecessary gamble fail was an almost certain watery grave and a bogey six. Discretion, in the shape of a lay-up short of the creek, an accurate chip and a single putt for a birdie four or even two for a par five, would have been by far the better part of valour.

But the adrenalin was flowing too strongly for clear thought. He stuck with his 4-wood and splashed the ball straight into Rae's Creek. He took six and finished a stroke behind that year's winner, Bernhard Langer. In other words, ladies and gentlemen, Curtis's course management was deficient. I thank you. There is a collection box near the door by which you leave, the proceeds from which will be used to drown the sorrows of the victims of Rae's Creek.

Wizard Prang, Old Boy

Air Force grounded by stray drive, Benin, 1987

Just no sense of humour, some of these civil service chappies. And you could tell the judge had never held a 3-iron in his life. Mathieu Boya must have felt a bit peeved to be popped into the slammer just for practising his golf. Mind you, as mishaps go, his was about as spectacular as you can get.

It's famously hazardous being a spectator at a tournament, particularly when ex-presidents of the USA are playing. Gerald Ford and George Bush Sr are just two who have done their darnedest to eliminate their former subjects with wayward shots once they no longer needed their votes. Bush went even further when, at the 1993 Doug Sanders Celebrity Classic in Texas – naturally – he winged his own vice-president, Dan Quayle (the man who famously was worried about visiting Latin America because he couldn't speak Latin). Some said it was fortunate Quayle survived, though not everybody was so sure.

But to destroy an entire national air force with one shot! Now that really *is* spectacular. Benin, in West Africa, is not a big country, so it doesn't need that large an air force. Five ageing Mirage jets seemed quite sufficient. Nor is Benin swarming with avid golf fanatics, and to make sure this remains the case there are no courses to play on. At least there weren't in 1987 when M Boya got into his swing and, since he proved just how dangerous a game golf can be, it's a reasonable bet there still aren't. Wishing to stay in good form, M Boya would take his clubs to a strip of waste ground and practise knocking a ball to and fro on that. As it happened, this bordered the airstrip used by the five Mirage jets, four of which were neatly parked in a

101

row at the time of the accident. The fifth was accelerating down the runway as M Boya had another whack at his ball.

He struck it well. It was undeniably a good shot but as it reached its zenith, a bird strayed into its path and both objects diverted rather sharply. The bird, being at best dazed and at worst dead, was unable to select its landing spot and dived beak first straight into the open cockpit of the Mirage gathering speed for takeoff. Quite why the pilot had his canopy open was not a thing the judge thought to ask. As it was, the pilot, unnerved, lost control of his plane, skidded into the other four and wrote off the lot. One would have thought this at least the equal of a hole in one and something that, in other circumstances, might produce an invitation to pop round and celebrate in the presidential palace. Alas, the Benin authorities were not imbued with a Battle of Britain spirit, and thought the prang a good deal less than wizard, seeing that the bill was around $40 million. Poor M Boya was promptly clapped into the nearest jail.

Azinger is Hunted Down

The Open, Muirfield, 1987

Even in the early days, Nick Faldo's presence exerted a very unsettling effect on his opponents. He has a considerable sense of humour, with a big store of jokes to swap with playing partners that he likes during the opening round of a tournament. Once the going gets serious, though, tunnel vision takes over, and Faldo's tight-lipped, brooding presence imposes itself.

His ferocious concentration seems to create anxiety in his opponents. For a decade they frequently gave the impression of being pursued by the Hound of the Baskervilles once they knew they were sharing the top of a leader board with him, and yet it was often the case that Nick was simply plugging away, getting par after relentless par. Perhaps that's where the problem lay – the knowledge gnawing at you that he was never going to make a mistake but was simply waiting for *you* to make one, just the one.

Paul Azinger was the first to crack in a major as he jousted with Faldo for the Auld Claret Jug at Muirfield in 1987. He started well, with rounds of 68 on each of the first two days, to hold a one-stroke lead over Nick. He held it through the third day as, playing together, both men battled the difficult conditions to achieve level par of 71, but Nick had noticed that, whereas Azinger was in control over the outward nine holes, he appeared to be less sure on the inward nine. Come the final day, damp and misty, Faldo went out with Craig Stadler ahead of Azinger and the South African David Frost. He never looked like missing par but, try as he might, he just could not register a birdie. On the ninth, he took a 3-iron, rather than a 4, and went right through the green, whereas Azinger had picked up two shots going out and was turning for home with a lead of three. It was all beginning to depend on whether he would blow up on the back nine.

Sure enough, by the time he reached the fateful seventeenth, Azinger had dropped the shots he had made on the first nine, and his lead was back to one stroke. At the 188-yard sixteenth, Faldo looked to have a wonderful chance of a birdie to draw level when he put his tee shot within six feet of the pin, yet still his putt wouldn't drop. The par-five seventeenth is a tough hole, but any player in contention is looking to get a birdie to screw the pressure onto his opponent, yet even here Faldo could not make it and had to be content with par. In his heart, he thought his chance of a first major title had gone.

Then came Azinger's big mistake. On the seventeenth tee he took out his driver against the wishes – indeed the pleadings, if not downright commands – of his caddie, Kevin Woodward, and drove the ball into the one spot no one playing the hole wants to be. He landed in a deep fairway bunker, carefully positioned to catch the careless drive. Once in, there is no way to come out and go forward at the same time. Like a crab, Azinger had to scuttle out sideways, missed the green with his third shot and then two-putted for a bogey six. He had lost his one-stroke lead and was all square as he came to the last, only for lightning to strike a second time.

It was his fairway shot that went astray on this occasion, a 5-iron planted firmly into a steep greenside bunker. Although he came out safely, he had left himself a long putt. In a brave and noble last effort he came within a whisker of holing it, but Faldo, in the scorer's hut, watched it stay out and knew himself to be Open champion for the first time.

The Muirfield crowd that day did not cover themselves in glory. They had watched Faldo come in, apparently unable to lift his game enough to seize the birdies that might have given him the clubhouse lead. Then, apparently from nowhere, Azinger began to drop back over the last couple of holes and his bad shots were cheered as though he were the one driving for victory. At the time, he seemed to take it philosophically. 'You can't help it,' he said. 'That's just life.' Yet it was noticeable that ever thereafter his matches with Faldo were tinged with a special intensity, as though he held him personally responsible for what happened that day.

A Little Ray of Sunshine

The Masters, Augusta, 1990

It's not a good idea to let little things prey on your mind. There are plenty of other things to worry about if you play golf, or any sport, at the highest level, and Ray Floyd, of all people, should have known it. By the time of his little spat with Britain's Nick Faldo he was a mature and worldly-wise 45 years old. A slow developer, despite winning his first major, the US PGA, at 27, he was 44 by the time he achieved his fourth and the one he most wanted, the US Open, becoming the oldest player to take that title.

One year later, in 1987, he was at the British Open at Muirfield (see page 103), playing the first two rounds in company with a couple of Nicks, Price and Faldo. As it happened, Price and Faldo were close friends who enjoyed each other's company and spent most of the first round swapping jokes. Maybe Floyd felt left out or maybe his sense of humour couldn't get the point of the banter (they may just have been bad jokes, of course) but they had barely left the first tee on the second day before An Incident occurred.

It was wet and miserable, which hardly helped, and Faldo started with two poor shots leaving himself a long and difficult third to the green to get away, as he hoped, with no worse than a bogey. He havered for some time over the right club, while Floyd waited on the green, getting steadily wetter. When Faldo finally played and walked up to where his partners were waiting, Floyd said: 'I thought you were never going to play that shot.'

It doesn't sound much to you or me. We put up with far worse than that most days of the week and think nothing of it. I suppose it depends

106

whether it's said with a grin or a scowl, but whatever sparked it in the first place, it heralded a lengthy period of strained relations. At the time, Faldo said nothing except to his caddie, Andy Prodger: 'The best way to treat that remark is to play well.' So he duly won the event.

Clearly, though, the incident rankled with both men, and Ryder Cup matches in 1987 and 1989 became a focal point for carrying it on. Since Faldo has won more points than any golfer in Ryder Cup history, poor old Ray could be said to have come off second best, especially since, as captain of the US team in 1989, he could do no better than draw, leaving the Cup in European hands after their historic win in America in 1987.

And so on to the 1990 Masters. After a third round of 66, young Mr Faldo (33) was three shots behind the leader, old Mr Floyd, by now topping 48. With a fourth round of 69, Nick forced a playoff for a chance to retain the green jacket he had won the previous year – after a playoff. So the ill-considered remark in the cold and wet of Muirfield three years earlier finally resolved itself into a one-to-one shootout in the evening sun on the second hole at Augusta, Georgia. Each had been Masters champion once, Floyd in 1976. Who would win the title for a second time? It did not take long to resolve the matter. The previous year, at this very same playoff hole, Scott Hoch had missed a putt from two feet under the basilisk gaze of Faldo. This time, Ray skimmed his second shot straight into the water. Augustan etiquette decreed he should shake hands with his nemesis as he conceded defeat, and with that he was free to look forward to a lucrative career on the Seniors Tour. The moral, if there is one, is that it's a bad idea to seek a grudge match against a younger player on the way up when you are nearing the end of your career.

Pizza to Go

US Women's Open,
Fort Worth, 1991

Luckily, there have always been some free spirits in the game of golf, and we need them more than ever as the so-called 'grit and grimace' brigade become ever more bowed under the weight of money and expectation. It was Walter Hagen who said, 'Don't worry. You're only here on a short visit, so don't forget to stop and smell the roses.' And he insisted this be engraved on his tombstone.

Hagen would have approved of Britain's Brian Barnes, a similarly free spirit in the 1960s and 1970s. In his day Barnes was a formidable golfer, who beat Jack Nicklaus twice in a day in the 1975 Ryder Cup, but he was never one to take golf, or life, too seriously. Coming to the last green of a tournament he was leading by four strokes, he once elected to mark his ball with a beer bottle (the contents of which had recently refreshed him). The rules state that a ball must be marked with a round object and in Barnes's opinion a bottle is undeniably round. 'Anyway, I knew that if they penalised me with a couple of strokes I'd still win.' The sponsors, who had supplied the refreshment, were delighted, but not the organisers – which bothered Barnes not one whit.

Like most of golf's free spirits, one of the things that bothered Barnes was stubbornly slow play. Suspecting what was in store during one European tour event, he stuffed a book and a folding canvas chair in his equipment and during holdups ahead of him, settled himself down for a good read on the tee or in the middle of the fairway.

Another pleasingly straightforward player, of whom Barnes and Hagen would approve, was Lori Garbacz, who began playing the US Ladies PGA tour in 1979. Despite being a superb player in an era of outstanding women players, Lori never quite dominated the scene, in part because she, too, could never quite bring herself to regard golf as the only important thing in life. If there was a little fun to be had along the way, she had it.

She shared Brian Barnes's impatience with slow play, and with the failure of tour officials to enforce the penalties available to them. In protest, she began to adopt similar tactics to the ones Barnes had used, most notably at the Mazda LPGA Championship. Whenever the pairing ahead went into a state of suspended animation, out would come a newspaper and a folding chair and down, very ostentatiously, she would sit, catching up on the state of the world in general and the stock market in particular. When the pair ahead felt it was safe to venture a little further forward, she would whack her ball down the fairway, lay up next to it and see what was on the next page.

The last straw, as far as Lori was concerned, came at the 1991 US Women's Open. It was, admittedly, brutally hot but even a ten-legged centipede could have got round Fort Worth's Colonial Country Club in quicker time. When she and her playing partner, plus their caddies and general attendants – agents, bank managers, fitness advisers, masseuses or whoever professional golfers have to have handy these days – reached the fourteenth hole they had had enough. One of them broke away to find a pay phone, called a local restaurant and ordered a pizza meal for the whole party. It was delivered as they arrived at the seventeenth, and they sat down to lunch to make their point in the grand manner.

Kiawah Capers

The Ryder Cup, Kiawah Island, 1991

It all depends how you look at it. Ask people to recall a golfing clanger and almost without thinking the majority nominate Bernhard Langer's missed putt in the 1991 Ryder Cup. It is, to say the least, unfair, given that it was a sufficiently testing shot for any player of any class to have missed in any situation. What made it *feel* like a clanger was the context. 'The War on the Shore' was what the American hype-makers chose to call the Ryder encounter that year, in keeping with the belligerent mood of the recent Gulf War.

Sam Ryder himself would have been appalled by the military forage caps the US team adopted, and by Paul Azinger's crass comment that having beaten the Iraqis it was time to beat the Europeans, especially given British fatalities in the same Gulf War, but it reflected American anxiety to get the Cup back after its six-year residence in Europe. Never in its 64-year history had the Americans been defeated on home soil except in 1987, and it was an insult that rankled. They did not want a repeat.

Generally, the four-ball and foursomes matches that occupy the first part of the Ryder Cup favour the Europeans, who are more at home in these kinds of contest. The thinking goes that this is where a lead of sufficient size has to be established before the Americans fight back in the singles, in which they no longer have to adopt the unusual, for them, posture of playing as a team. So, when the Kiawah singles began on the final day with the score 8–8, things looked pretty hairy for Britain and Europe. Unusually, only eleven singles were scheduled because Steve Pate had been injured in a car crash a few days earlier, and, although he partnered Corey Pavin in the four-balls, and lost, he withdrew from further endeavour. He had originally been slated to meet Seve Ballesteros and that – since Seve never willingly loses to anyone, and assuredly not to an American – meant a half-point forfeited once it was agreed to regard the unplayed match as a tie.

If the Europeans had once been anxious about playing on American soil they had long since lost the feeling. The singles turned out to be a real dogfight and it all came down to the last green of the last match. Hale Irwin had been leading Bernhard Langer, but when it comes to slugging it out Bernhard can hold his own against the best. With the scores standing at thirteen and a half points each, Irwin sank his last putt for a bogey, leaving Langer with a seven-foot putt (or six-foot, five-foot, four-foot – as time passes the putt gets shorter and shorter in the retelling) to level the match, keep the overall score tied at 14–14 and ensure the Cup remained with the Europeans.

It was José María Olazábal who once said about the Ryder, 'I promise you, everything is shaking apart from the shaft of your club – and that's before you take it out of the bag.' But Langer has been tested in countless fires, and not one single member of the European team doubted that he was the man for the job. For the first six and a half feet of its journey, his putt looked certain to fall and then, at the last moment, it swung the merest shade to the right, kissed the rim and stayed out. None of the players thought it was a clanger, and nor should we.

One of These Days You'll Drive Me Too Far

Denver Airport, 1994; Texas Open, 1952; Braids Tournament, 1913

Among modern players John Daly is not a man you would expect to come up short with a driver in his hands. He was once led out to the middle of Denver Airport and invited to give the ball a bit of tap, with the result that it pitched on the tarmac at 360 yards, took a friendly bounce and skittered playfully on for a further 450 before coming to rest, exhausted. That made a total length of 810 yards, just 70 yards short of half a mile.

When Daly turned up for the 1994 Masters he found they had taken the precaution of adding a further 65 feet to the top of the netting on the practice ground, which was already 260 yards from the practice tees. As you would expect, this was inviting trouble. In no time, bets were being placed on (a) whether big John could clear the netting, and/or (b) how many attempts it would take him to do it. The answer was three.

Carl Cooper couldn't quite match Daly's 810 yards when he drove from the third tee in the 1952 Texas Open at Oak Hills, but he came close. The only snag was that it didn't do a lot for his chances of a good score, let alone winning the tournament. He struck the ball cleanly, if not all that straight, and wouldn't have been too displeased with his effort in its early stages. Unfortunately, a cart track ran alongside the hole; even more unfortunately, the earth in the middle of a Texan summer was rock hard; and yet more unfortunately, Carl's ball landed on the cart track. With all the persistence of Ol' Man River, it kept on going in direct ratio to the speed with which his hopes and his spirits went on sinking. It finally stopped at an impressive 780 yards. The hole, on the other hand, was a trifling 470 or so, meaning that poor old Carl now had to fashion an approach shot to carry over 300 yards and, having walked well over a third of a mile to catch up with his ball, he wasn't quite up to it.

Had he been around at the time, George Russell would have lent him a sympathetic shoulder to cry on. At the Braids Tournament in 1913, Mr Russell had scrambled up the slope to the tee, set his ball up nice and high to clear the rough before him, surveyed the fairway beyond and now began a good, steady backswing. Regrettably, he managed to hit the ball as he took the club back, rolled it off the back of the tee platform and watched it gather speed down the steep hill up which he had just puffed and panted, coming to rest 300 yards away to set an unofficial record for the longest drive backwards. Like Carl Cooper's, his spirits must have sunk, but in those days help was probably at hand. No doubt he reached for his hip flask and simply topped them up again.

How to Double Your Weight and Win The Open

The Open, St Andrews, 1995

This chapter shouldn't be here, it really shouldn't, but it's irresistible. When big John Daly (and by big I mean what I say – see page 126) weighed in for the 1995 Open at the Royal and Ancient he had been off the bottle for two years. He would never lose the universal tag of 'The Wild Thing' that his predilection for drinking and gambling had pinned on him, but 1995 was one of his years for good golf and chocolate-chip muffins. He came to St Andrews determined on two things: this was his course, and he was going to use his formidable driver at every possible opportunity. 'I'm really going for it this week,' he told his caddie. 'I'm going to win this thing.' He knew the Old Course gave him room to shorten its distance provided he kept long, left and out of trouble, most of which lay to the right. He did what he set out to do, and did it brilliantly, holding off a strong field and beating Constantino Rocca in a playoff.

This chapter is not about his golf. There was nothing but praise for that. It's more concerned with solving the mystery of how a top sportsman can put on weight when he's at full throttle beating his challengers. You would have thought that the effort of all those practice sessions, the requirement to walk four or five miles per round, and the pressures and mental tension that cause the metabolism to overheat would leave a man weak with effort, and an exposed ribcage to rival that of a patient whose doctor has kept him off solids for a month. With a normal man, perhaps, but not if your name's John Daly.

His idea of a light snack over which to wind down in the evening consisted of as many steaks as the local hostelries could muster washed down with oodles of ice cream. Fair enough. Biffing a golf ball with the unrestrained vigour of a Daly takes it out of you. It was all the secret snacks as he trundled around the course that were the giveaway, indulging what at times seemed more like a picnic walk with occasional interludes for swatting a small ball prodigious distances. Chocolate-chip muffins were John's particular thing, and I only hope his faithful caddie, Greg Rita, got a handsome reward at the end of the tournament because he worked beyond the normal call.

On the one hand there was the usual club handling, advice and general whatnot, but on the other there was the constant demand for chocolate-chip muffins. At times he felt like a waiter in a restaurant. 'Driver and two muffins, and make it quick.' A cache of the luxurious goodies was established behind the tenth, but with The Open in progress you can't forever be dashing across the course on raiding missions, and there's only so much room in a golf bag, what with all the other items that have to be stowed.

Crisis point was reached towards the end of the third round as supplies teetered on the edge of exhaustion and, possibly in consequence, Daly lost his lead to fall four shots behind. Relief, though, was at hand. The Scots are famed for never missing a money-making opportunity, and word of Mr Daly's secret passion had leaked out. That very night a box was delivered to the Old Course hotel, where he was staying. By morning, the box was empty but Daly was happy. He stormed onto the course and into history, and as he lifted the Cup he was a heavier and a happier man.

'I Got My Behind Whipped'

The Masters, Augusta, 1996

In a court of law Nick Faldo might, in other circumstances, have gone down for a long spell at Her Majesty's Pleasure. Not for GBH – though it's true he was armed with some brutal-looking clubs at the time, not to mention a pretty formidable-looking caddie by the name of Fanny – but more for GMH, or grievous mental harm. As far as we can tell, he didn't pick on Greg Norman deliberately. Put him alongside a playing partner with whom he was in contention for a title and, no matter that there was never a trace of blood to be found, his opponent generally finished feeling he'd been bludgeoned with a 5-iron – or a driver, a putter, a sand wedge or any other club with which Faldo could inflict damage.

For Norman, the Great White Shark, the problem in confronting Faldo in the final round of the 1996 Augusta Masters was that he'd already suffered once before, in the 1990 Open at St Andrews. On that occasion the two had played the final round together and Faldo had come from behind to relieve him of the major that Greg believed must surely be his after so many years of coming close. But this Masters was different. Wasn't it? Norman had twice been runner-up, so he was wiser and steadier now and the six-stroke lead he held as the pair teed off for the final round was surely impregnable. Surely. Moreover, Faldo's second marriage had collapsed and he had failed to finish near the top in his previous eight majors. This time it seemed clear that fate had cast Faldo as Norman's train-bearer for the progression around Augusta to his coronation.

That was not, of course, the way Faldo saw it. In those days, only golf mattered to him, and in the days before the Masters he analysed and tinkered, adjusted and practised his short game, his putting in particular. Now he decided to 'stand tall' as he putted, using shoulders rather than arms. It was to make a crucial difference, but if Norman had not started so carelessly – or so nervily – Faldo would not have had the chance to bleed the Shark white with his newly recovered accuracy around the greens.

Norman handed Faldo the psychological advantage from the very first hole. He pitched his second shot over a tree into a bunker and three-putted. By the turn, Faldo was within two strokes and on the eleventh green catastrophe struck. Putting for a birdie, Norman missed, went well past the hole and missed the return, taking three putts to put the ball away. Then came the twelfth.

'That', said Faldo, 'was like good old matchplay. I had to go first and it's difficult to hit that shallow green. But I did, and the pressure was on Greg.'

Norman put his ball in the water, took five and, from being six up at the start, was now two behind. At the fifteenth, he made a brave play for an eagle but finished with a birdie – and so did Faldo. The *coup de grâce* came at the short sixteenth, where he took a 6-iron and hooked the ball straight into the water.

As the pair walked from the eighteenth green, they draped their arms round each other's shoulders. It was a rare display of emotion for Faldo on a golf course and he feared – with every justification, as it proved – that the final round would be remembered not for his marvellous 67 but for Norman's spectacular collapse. Worse has happened in the history of major championships, even to the great Arnie Palmer in the 1966 US Open (see page 76), but rarely in the face of such intense media expectation.

The Great White Shark was philosophy itself in the aftermath. However much he may have wanted to lock himself in the Butler Cabin and weep, he was brave and forthright in front of the cameras. 'I made a lot of mistakes and I blame myself completely. But I'll wake up in the morning; I'll still be breathing. God, I'd love to be putting on a green jacket but my life is going to continue. I've got forty million bucks.'

Well, yes, I suppose that does help to deaden the pain of converting a six-stroke lead into a five-shot deficit.

When Is a Son Not a Son?

Burhill GC's annual family foursomes, 1996

As World War Two approached its end, Burhill Golf Club in Surrey had a brilliant idea: an annual Family Foursomes. The rules governing entry were soon run off and ever since it has been, as it continues to be, an enjoyable event. From far and wide it attracts parents with their sons and daughters, their handicaps ranging from the eyebrow-raising to the mind-boggling, as was always intended.

The 52nd Family Foursomes, however, ran into a spot of bother – not out on the course, but after it was all over and everyone had, as ever, enjoyed themselves. Audrey Briggs, winner of four Welsh amateur titles, was playing with her thirteen-year-old son Laurie. They won their first two rounds before losing in the third and later wrote to the club to thank them for hosting the event. Mrs Briggs was surprised by the reply she received, indicating that she and Laurie had been ineligible in the first place and should not have been competing. So what on earth went wrong?

According to the club, stepchildren were debarred from entering the Family Foursomes (a strange rule, but no problems so far since Laurie was not a stepson). But there was more. Adopted children, it continued, *should* have been debarred. Nobody had thought to say so in the rules of entry, but that would all be put right in time for the next Family Foursomes, so Mrs Briggs and Laurie could relax and not worry about playing the following year. It was indeed the case that Laurie was adopted – shortly after he was born – but the rule seemed at best odd and at worst unfair.

Members' collars, or what lay under them, began to heat up quite rapidly. There was nothing in writing to say that only blood relations were allowed to enter, and reliance on folk memory going back over fifty years was most unsatisfactory. Even had such evidence been found, it seemed clear to the majority that conditions and attitudes at the end of the twentieth century made the ban unacceptable, the more so by the time the R&A became involved. So the stipulations were withdrawn, Audrey Briggs and Laurie were invited back for the next Family Foursomes and bygones soon became bygones.

Come On In,
the Water's Lovely

The Open, Carnoustie, 1999

Golf being an individual game, you are mercilessly exposed to clangers. Short of burying yourself in a pot bunker or refusing to come out of the gorse bushes, there is no hiding place when things go wrong. Alternatively, you can make a virtue of misfortune and defiantly flaunt it to the world.

Jean van der Velde unwittingly took the latter route as he reached with both hands and, for that matter, bare feet, for the Auld Claret Jug on the eighteenth hole of the final round of the 1999 Open at Carnoustie. The sight of van der Velde, trousers rolled above his knees, paddling in the Barry Burn while contemplating a submarine shot must be the best-publicised clanger in golfing history.

Four days earlier, van der Velde had been a 150–1 outsider for the Open, but by the time he started his final round he had a three-stroke lead. There was only the usual question: would this relative unknown buckle under the pressure, as so many had done before? Over the first eight of the outward nine, the answer seemed to be yes, as he dropped three shots, but on the ninth tee a voice from the crowd shouted, 'Keep your head up, Jean.' 'Yes,' replied Jean looking round, and was as good as his word. Uncertainty was thrown off, and, by the time he stood on the eighteenth tee, a 487-yard, par-four, he could afford to take a double-bogey six and still win.

With such a lead Nick Faldo, and many another professional, would have taken an iron off the tee and played safe for par. Van der Velde took a driver and hit it cleanly, but it was the second that began the comedy of errors, 'a performance straight out of an anarchic French circus', as Paul Hayward wrote in the *Telegraph*. He tried to fly his second all the way to the green, but pushed the ball well to the right and watched it hit the stand and ricochet into the deep chasm of the Barry Burn, still a good chip away from the green.

That was the point at which things really got out of hand, as van der Velde splashed around the burn without benefit of bucket and spade, the omnipresent, ever-hungry TV cameras relaying every protracted move to the watching millions around the world. 'Just wait a bit longer, the tide's going out,' advised his playing partner Craig Parry, unhelpfully but with deadly prescience, since the next act in the drama would involve building sandcastles. Van der Velde eventually returned to dry land for his fifth shot, still with a chance of a chip and a putt to get down in six and claim the title. With hideous inevitability, he flopped it straight into a bunker and yet, needing a seven-foot putt to register seven and at least qualify for a three-way playoff, pulled his shattered nerves together with something approaching heroism to sink it.

As night follows day, he shanked his first playoff shot into the gorse, and Paul Lawrie, who had started the final round ten shots behind, emerged as the new Open champion. 'God', Hayward wrote, 'combined a hero and a headcase in one incomparable package and sent him to play golf at Carnoustie.'

Van der Velde himself tended to agree. 'Yes, I have the red nose in my bag,' he said afterwards. He also said his aim in playing golf was to promote the game and entertain people, and he triumphantly achieved both – though at what personal cost we can never fully realise. The monetary penalty of blowing £320,000 is clear enough, but the inner self-belief is something entirely different.

The Brookline Bear Pit

The Ryder Cup, Brookline, 1999

Sam Ryder learned his golf from Abe Mitchell (who was thought by many of his contemporaries to be the best golfer never to have won The Open), and was so impressed by the sporting spirit displayed by the teams in a meeting between British and American teams at Wentworth in 1926 that he donated the Ryder Cup. The Battle of Brookline in 1999, the Bear Pit as it was almost immediately dubbed, would have horrified him.

The seeds of warning were sown in 1979 when Europe, rather than just Britain and Ireland, began to compete for the Cup with America and, in 1985, introduced the latter to the novel idea of being beaten. It then rubbed salt in the wound by hanging onto the Cup for the next six years. American culture recognises only winners, a dangerous concept since in any sporting contests losers must necessarily always outnumber winners. The Ryder Cup at Kiawah Island in 1991, coming shortly after the Gulf War, was distastefully dubbed the 'War on the Shore', and the behaviour of crowd and players alike was not the best advertisement golf had ever received. But Brookline was another matter altogether.

David Duval got things off to a bad start in 1999 by dismissing his selection for the US team not as an honour but as a requirement to play in 'an exhibition', for which he should be paid. This seemed to many a case of the rich forsaking national pride in order to get richer. Payne Stewart was also sufficiently ill-advised to assert that the European players were not fit to caddie for the American stars, which rather overlooked the fact that the last time the European team had contested the Cup on

American soil in 1995, it had come away victorious. By the penultimate evening of the Brookline meeting, Europe led 10–6 with the twelve singles to follow, therefore needing four and a half points on the final day to be sure of victory. But the singles are generally America's strongest card and although they seemed drained of morale the night before, overnight they discovered a team spirit that Duval's earlier remarks had suggested would be beyond them.

On the final day they played superbly, and whatever may be said of subsequent events nothing should be allowed to detract from one of the great sporting fightbacks from adversity. It was not the *fact* of victory but the *manner* of it that left such an alarming taste in people's mouths. Part of the trouble arose from the fact that 40,000 spectators were crammed into areas that could scarcely accommodate 25,000, the more normal number of tickets given out for Ryder Cup matches.

For whatever reason, the behaviour of the overcrowded terraces and walkways seemed normal only to those who were more accustomed to soccer terraces. Colin Montgomerie suffered such a string of shouted insults and gibes that his father left the playing area in distress. Jane James, wife of the nonplaying captain Mark James, was spat at, not once but several times, and things were barely any better in the clubhouse among the well-heeled New England members watching on television.

Out on the course the scene was set, almost inevitably, by Duval. As he took the fourteenth hole to defeat Jasper Parnevik 4 and 5, to give the US its sixth singles win and a 12–10 lead with six matches still out on the course, he ran round the green with his hand cupped to his ear encouraging the crowd to shout louder. And this was the man who was being dragged unwillingly onto the course to play a meaningless exhibition?

The worst came in the ninth match, between Justin Leonard and José María Olazábal. On the seventeenth green Leonard sank a 40-foot putt with Olazábal still to play. The match and the destiny of the Cup was technically still in the balance but, presumably under the impression they had already won, the following US players and their wives and, it seemed, half the American nation, poured all over the green – and Olazábal's line to the pin – in a war dance of triumph. Not surprisingly, José María had no hope of dropping his putt on the indented green that resulted, though he did manage to halve the match.

In the match behind, Payne Stewart was so appalled by the behaviour of the crowd and its treatment of Monty, his long-suffering opponent, that to his eternal credit he conceded an eighteen-foot putt on the last green to give him the game. The US had an unassailable lead by then but it was a gesture that restored some honour to the proceedings.

Michael Bonnalack of the R&A, present as a guest, said he was 'embarrassed for the game of golf', and Jane James, once she had cleaned herself up, feared for the possibility of retaliation when the US team came to the Belfry for the next Ryder Cup in 2001 (which in the event proved to be 2002). 'I would hate it if we lowered ourselves to that kind of level.' She need not have worried. By then, repentance had taken firm hold, and the behaviour, ecstatic as it was at the return of the Cup to Europe, was impeccable.

'Get Me to the Airport, Fast'

US Open, Pebble Beach, 2000

However you look at him, John Daly comes in one shape only: outsize. Added to which the concept of doing things by halves is beyond his comprehension or experience. Marriages? Line 'em up. Divorces? Ditto (his second wife nearly gave the ageing Augusta committeemen collective apoplexy when she sprang from the bushes during a practice round at the 1993 Masters to serve divorce papers on Daly).

His relationship with the bottle is as on/off as his marriages. He once had a lucrative sponsorship deal with Callaway Golf, who wrote into his contract a clause banning him from liquor and requiring him to take daily doses of Prozac and assorted antidepressants. John abandoned the pills and the contract in September 1999. 'It was giving me headaches, diarrhoea and making me bloated,' he explained, turning to beer and vodka to replace his previous love affair with Jack Daniel's. As for weight, by the end of 2003, Daly weighed in around 282 pounds (that's 20 stone in real money), before subsiding to a wraith-like 238 pounds (at a mere 17 stone you could miss him if he was standing behind the flag) for the start of the 2004 golf season, the next crop of Thanksgiving turkeys not yet being oven-ready.

There is, of course, an advantage in being solidly built: the ball travels like a rocket-propelled grenade when you strike it. For such an explosive hitter, though, Daly can be delicate around the greens. The problem, in keeping with his lifetime inability to do anything in moderation, is that when things go wrong they go sensationally wrong. In the 1999 US Open at Pinehurst he had been leading in the final round when he collided with a septuple bogey on the par-four eighth. He swore with Shakespearian directness never to play the US Open again. In the 2000 US Open at Pebble Beach he opened with a respectable round of three over par, but this time it was the final hole of the second round where things went spectacularly pear-shaped.

The par-five eighteenth at Pebble Beach is picturesque – or at least it was until it came under siege from Daly. He opened with a monster slice into the backyard of someone's house, which, very wisely, was ruled to be out of bounds. You can't have the Open going through your garden when you're trying to get the barbecue alight. He decided to have another go from the tee and corrected the slice so well that he hooked drives two and three into the Pacific Ocean, to the consternation of several flatfish dozing on the bottom.

Belatedly deciding discretion was the better part of valour, he next turned to his 5-iron and trundled the ball modestly down the fairway, before chipping short of the green with his eighth shot. Number nine nearly followed its cousins into the Pacific but fell into a hazard instead, allowing Daly a drop. Unfortunately, the drop finished at the foot of a wall, forcing the maestro to play his tenth shot left-handed – into a bunker. By this stage the gallery was in a state of semi-hysterical tension wondering where he'd find to put it next, but they needn't have worried. He blasted out with aplomb, two-putted for 14, signed his card for an 83 and legged it before he could be arrested for abusing a golf course. 'Get me to the airport, fast,' he was alleged to have told a taxi driver, but can this be true? Daly hates flying and drives everywhere in his own motor home. For one thing, none of his wives can get at him there and, as he says, 'You get in a plane and get a little diet Coke with a half-plastic cup. The food tastes bad and you can't smoke. I can't stand it.'

Rules Are Made to Be Broken – But Not in Golf

More tales of long-suffering caddies, 2001

It really is amazing how much a caddie has to put up with. Quite apart from humping half a ton of high-tech metal several thousand yards every day, he's expected to know when to chatter like a chimpanzee or imitate a Trappist monk; take any amount of abuse when his lord and master has made a Horlicks of it; know at any given second precisely how many miles, yards or feet it is to the pin and be accurate to within half an inch; know at all times precisely how many clubs are in the bag and of what sort – and to catch like Marcus Trescothick in the slips.

Why should he have reflexes so fast they would make a cheetah look slow? Because he whose every whim must be obeyed is liable to hurl the club or the ball in his general direction without warning and possibly without looking. Missed the putt. Damnation. Hurl the putter away – bound to be a caddy around somewhere to catch it. Which is all very well, but the consequences can be serious, especially if there's a lake in the vicinity.

At the Forest of Arden in 2001, Raymond Russell tossed his ball to his caddie. He may have had an irresistible urge to see him dive full length while carrying a large bag on his back, but we shall never know. What we do know is that his caddie missed it, and with a carefree bound the ball settled into the bottom of a passing lake. Did Mr Russell order him to take off his shoes and wade in after it? Right first time, but however many layers the caddie peeled off, and however deep he dived, of the ball there was no further sight. And for this, the rules decree a penalty of two strokes. It makes you question the origin of rules. At what point in the mist-filled past was there a player with such a penchant for holding up the game while he hurled golf balls into the lake that it was felt necessary to introduce such a penalty?

Long before that, one of the best-known caddies on the circuit, Dave Musgrove, was carrying the bags for American Lee Janzen, who had just chipped onto the green. Janzen marked his ball and tossed it to Musgrove to buff up a bit. Unfortunately, he didn't realise Musgrove was looking straight into the sun and, although he held out a hopeful hand in the general direction, the ball hit him and bounced away. A green is, by and large, a difficult place on which to lose all track of a white ball, but peer as they might it was nowhere to be seen.

After a while, the only remaining option seemed to be that it had bounced into the open pocket of Janzen's golf bag, standing on the edge of the green. They peered inside, to be greeted with a vista of spankingly white and pristine golf balls, the majority with the identical number to the one in play. Musgrove spread the lot out and examined them one by one until he came to his eureka moment. On one was a tiny piece of grass and that, thankfully for Janzen and Musgrove alike, was what saved the day.

'You're Going to Go Ballistic'

The Open, Royal Lytham, 2001

Caddies may frequently feel like members of Her Majesty's Opposition at Westminster, in a position where they can't win however right they are. But just occasionally one of them drops a horrendous clanger. Curtis Strange, for example, was quietly going about his business at the Jackie Gleason Inverrary Classic in 1979 and was walking across a bridge to the ninth tee with his caddie, Mark Freiburg, tottering along obediently in his wake. Suddenly, there was noise, a muffled curse and a series of splashes behind him, and he turned to see most of his clubs vanishing into the water as Freiburg lost his footing. Nobly resisting the temptation to toss his caddie after them, Strange played on with the putter and three irons that had resisted drowning.

If Freiburg felt chastened, what can have gone through the head of Myles Byrne, caddying for Ian Woosnam at the 2001 Open, as he walked down the first fairway in the final round and realised there were fifteen clubs in the bag instead of the regulation fourteen? It wouldn't have been so bad had Woosie been conforming to his usual Open habits. In twenty attempts, he had finished in the top ten on only four occasions, but this was different. At the age of 43 he was the leader at the end of the third round, his 67 putting him level on 207 with Bernhard Langer, Alex Cejka and the eventual winner, David Duval. Overnight, Woosnam admitted in an interview, 'I am in love with golf. Anybody who is British wants to win this championship. There's a lot at stake, but I'm not putting pressure on myself.' True. He let others do it for him.

Woosie had been worrying all week about the quality of his woods off the tee, and before the final round spent some time on the practice ground experimenting with a different driver. That's where things began to go wrong. Both the old and the new driver wanted to go round Lytham with him, so they both jumped into the bag together. Blissfully unaware, Woosnam started the final round like a Ferrari on the grid. He took out his 6-iron at the par-three first and for most of its flight his drive seemed to be heading for a hole in one before finishing a few inches short of the cup for a birdie two and a magical start to his assault on the title he wanted so much.

As he followed Woosnam down the first, poor Myles Byrne must have been tempted, as he tumbled to the awful truth of the situation, to creep into the rough and bury the offending extra club but, that failing, his only option was to break the news. Clearing his throat hopefully he sidled up to the man who probably wasn't going to tip him overgenerously when the truth came out and said, with a flash of prophecy, 'Ian, you're going to go ballistic. We've [note the use of the "we"] got two drivers in the bag.'

Woosie, normally the most cheerful and generous of souls, duly went ballistic. On the second tee the match referee, John Paramore, confirmed the disastrous news that the sin was indeed beyond what a normal mortal could know or understand, the penalty for which was an additional two strokes – i.e. he had not landed a brilliant birdie at the first to leap into an early lead, but had bogied it to slip off the top of the board. The offending extra club, still warm and comfy in its head cover, was promptly hurled across the second tee and left for others to retrieve.

Not surprisingly, Woosie played the next couple of holes with the air of a man distracted before bravely pulling himself together and getting an eagle at the sixth hole. He finished in joint third place with a round of 71 and an aggregate of 278, four strokes behind the winner.

Howard's Masterclass

Sawgrass, 2001

The par-three seventeenth on the Stadium Course at Sawgrass, USA, has undone more than a few of golf's big names during the annual Players Championship on the PGA tour. In the 2002 meeting it did for Craig Stadler, who admitted, 'The golf course got up and bit me in the arse' as he double-bogeyed it. It's a watery classic, the green consisting of a small island in the middle of a lake guarded at the front by a lone pot bunker. From the tee, it's generally an 8- or 9-iron shot, though in spring the erratic cross-breezes make club selection a headache. It's the kind of hole that preys on the mind long before you reach it.

Being the 17th, or 71st in a four-round tournament, it is the penultimate hole to be played and therefore one that can dash the hopes of a title if you mess up. As the 2002 Players Champion, Craig Perks, admitted, 'I'm thinking about it ten holes before I get to it. You can see some of the most horrendous shots there you've ever seen from some of the best players in the world.' In other words, it's a hole made for golfing clangers, though not of the kind committed by Yorkshire's Howard Clark.

Howard was unlikely to be unduly dismayed as he confronted Sawgrass's dreaded seventeenth in front of the TV cameras. He was, after all, six times a Ryder Cup player and one of the heroes of the epic 1985 battle at the Belfry before he withdrew from competitive golf to become a radio and TV commentator. His new employers stationed him on the seventeenth tee at Sawgrass armed with a couple of dozen golf balls and a club or two, trained the cameras on him and gave him the green light to demonstrate just how easy it is to get the hole horribly wrong.

Howard indicated that the challenge was mental and explained how easy the hole would be if only it was surrounded by grass, not water. He pointed out the hazards, advising that the thing to do was ignore the flag and concentrate on landing the ball on the green to give yourself a putting chance, even if it was from 25 or 30 feet. He even illuminated the golfer's mind with the thought that it could be a relief to roll back into the pot bunker because at least you were still alive, and not in the water under penalty.

And, so saying, he put the first ball down to start demonstrating the many things that could assail the best of golfers on the seventeenth. With an easy swing, the ball climbed into the blue sky as viewers gripped the arms of their sofas to see if he was intending to illustrate the flop into the bunker or to show how easily one could overshoot into the water on the far side of the little island. The ball reached its zenith and began to arc gracefully downwards. It landed smack in the middle of the green, bounced once and rolled apologetically into the cup for a hole in one. Hell and damnation! Why had he given up tournament golf so early?

'I Don't Play Well When I'm Not Having Fun'

Players Championship, Sawgrass, 2002 and 2004

What drives the many professionals who devote their lives to golf? Is it the potential fame, the money or the sheer enjoyment of playing the game? If they're very lucky it's all three, of course, but when one sees the harrowing tension frozen into many of their faces, it's a relief to encounter the one or two for whom the pleasure of playing the game matters most. José María Olazábal had a disappointing third round in the 2002 Benson and Hedges International Open and said, 'It was a lovely day out there. The sun was shining, there was a nice breeze, the birds were singing.' But what about his round? they asked. 'Oh, the golf. That was ******* awful!'

In April 2004, Phil Mickelson finally lost his tag of the best golfer never to have won a major. He certainly looked pretty chuffed as he was helped into his green jacket at Augusta, but Phil, more than most, epitomises the golfer for whom enjoying the game is the single most important thing. It is not for nothing that Arnold Palmer, being an instinctive gambler, is one of Mickelson's great heroes. The buzz of pulling off a series of impossible shots outweighed the disappointment of fluffing a championship.

There is a tale of Mickelson's disappearing into the woods in a tournament at Tucson, Arizona. His caddie handed him an 8-iron with which to try to extract himself from his spot of bother. Mickelson tossed it back and took a 3-iron, skimmed the ball off the nearby lake with a couple of bounces, flew it through a gap between two banks and onto the green. When his caddie had got his breath back he asked Mickelson why he had immediately cursed so loudly. 'I was trying for three bounces off the lake,' he said.

On that occasion, Phil got away with it, but there have been numerous occasions when things went the other way. In 2001 at Pebble Beach he blew a tournament he was leading by carting his drive at the eighteenth straight into the Pacific Ocean (though he's hardly the first to have done that – see page 126). Only the week before the 2002 Players Championship at Sawgrass, he had lost another tournament when he failed to resist the challenge of curling his ball round a wood that was hoping to grow up to be a forest and landed in the middle of a lake.

Now here he was in the third round at Sawgrass, tucked in just behind the leaders. It was at the seventh that things began to veer, literally, off course. First he pulled his drive into the trees, then he misjudged two attempted chips and found himself well over the green. He dropped off the lead a bit. That was as nothing to what awaited him at the tenth, where he did not exactly cover himself with glory in getting to the green but, nevertheless, could have saved par with a halfway decent putt. At this point he seemed, not for the first time in his career, to lose his presence of mind. He forgot golf and opted instead for a spot of hockey. He sent his first putt six feet past the pin. His second reduced the deficit to four feet, at which point he just stayed on the move, biffing the ball back and forth and ending up with a quadruple bogey.

'Unprofessional,' huffed the reporters, 'humiliating.' But Phil was disarmingly undismayed. 'I need to be creative, I need to attack,' he said afterwards. 'If it's no fun, I don't enjoy it. I am not going to play this game without the enjoyment, without the fun.'

Good for you, Phil. We need more like you – and congratulations on nailing the Masters in 2004.

'I Can Win on This Course'

The Open, Muirfield, 2002

There are gaffes, and there are bigger gaffes – those occasions when the mouth is opened wide and you watch with fascinated helplessness as the foot is rammed into it. The Muirfield home of the Honourable Company of Edinburgh Golfers draws forth plenty of praise from those who see golf as a test of accuracy and shot-making rather than brute force. Nick Price, Colin Montgomerie and David Toms were quick to sing its praises at the halfway stage of the 2002 Open, but on mature reflection Toms and Monty in particular probably wished they hadn't.

Price was scathing about the modern tendency to try to make a golf course harder simply by making it longer. 'That doesn't make a golf course harder. All it does is make the game more of a smash from the tee and I feel that's the wrong way to go,' he said. 'In the US Open and the Masters I don't have a prayer unless I get a bazooka for a driver.'

Irishman Des Smyth agreed, as he briefly took the tournament lead from Price at the end of the second day. 'There's no advantage for the power hitters at Muirfield,' he explained. 'It plays right into the hands of the straight hitters.'

Montgomerie also agreed: 'The best setup we have in major championship golf right now.'

Most enthusiastic of all was David Toms, the US PGA champion, who led the Muirfield Open at the end of Day One. 'I can play this style of golf,' he said. 'Every year I've gone back to Augusta, and they've done something to the course to play away from my hands. And the US Open definitely wasn't for me. But I can win on this course.'

Now let's take a look at what happened to the three great proponents of giving good, accurate, shot-making golfers a proper course, such as Muirfield, to play on. Nick Price did well, finishing three strokes behind the winner, Ernie Els, with rounds of 68, 70, 75 and 68. Boast fulfilled, I think we can say. Monty's bogey struck again, but we're used to that by now. His aggregate of 297 was 19 more than the winner's, made up of 74, 64 (very good), 84 (very bad) and 75 (very medium).

Now it is quite true that the third day's weather was terrible – 'storm-tossed', the papers called it – and Monty was not the only one to suffer (Tiger Woods captured the major headlines with 81), but surely the thinking straight shooters are the ones who should cope better with bad weather than the slam-it-'n'-see brigade. Gary Evans from Sussex managed a third-round 74 in the conditions and finished The Open only one shot behind the winner, so it must be possible.

Whatever one thinks, Monty vanished from the course with an impressive turn of speed after his 84, and on the following day gave the press boys a real working over for saying he had stormed off. 'I didn't,' he said, before leaving them dumbstruck with his next comment: 'I haven't shown any sign of temper on a golf course for five years.'

And last, and probably also least, we come to David Toms, whose first-round 67 had made him reckon *he* could win on this course. His next three rounds were 75, 81 and 75 for an aggregate 298 and 83rd position or – to put it more brutally – last. Oh, well. There's always next year – so long as it's not Muirfield again.

Curtis Gets a Strange Feeling

The Ryder Cup, the Belfry, 2002

'With 24 of the best players in the world, anyone can beat anyone on any given day,' said Bernhard Langer, playing in his tenth Ryder Cup. This sense of parity was underlined at the end of the four-balls and foursomes when the score, as at Kiawah Island in 1991 (see page 110) stood all-square at 8–8. Once again, things did not look good for the Europeans, singles being, supposedly, America's strongest suit. But when two armies are roughly equal it's the quality of the generals that counts.

Curtis Strange was captaining the US team, and the evening before the critical final day he pondered his playing order for the twelve singles. On paper, the Americans looked to be favourites. In Tiger Woods and Phil Mickelson he had players rated numbers one and two in the world, while the Europeans had players, such as Ireland's Paul McGinley and the Welshman Philip Price (rated 119 in the world), who appeared to be there mainly to make up the numbers. He decided to follow the accepted practice and open with his less strongly fancied names, building in strength and formidable reputation all the way down the list to Tiger, who would come out at number twelve.

On the other side of town, Sam Torrance was stroking his moustache with one hand, and reaching for his pint with the other, as he debated the same question. Finally, he made up his mind. He would go the high-risk route. His first five would be his strongest and most battle-hardened veterans: Colin Montgomerie, Sergio Garcia, Darren Clarke, Bernhard Langer and Padraig Harrington. Price would go in at number eleven against Mickelson, and Jesper Parnevik at twelve against Woods. When Curtis looked at the list a strange feeling came over him. 'I know why Sam's done that,' he said. 'He wants to get the spectators involved early. He wants to get momentum going and he wants to feed it over into the back end of the field.' Got it in one, Curtis.

Things worked out exactly as Sam Torrance had intended. Curtis Strange could only watch with a sinking feeling in his stomach that ripened into a fully blown tummy-ache as Montgomerie led off with a blistering demolition of Scott Hoch. 'I followed Sam's instructions,' he said. By the fourteenth green he had finished his day's work, and all the way back round the course European adrenalin flowed faster while American anxiety increased. Langer saw off Hal Sutton 4 and 3, Clarke halved his game, Harrington romped home by 5 and 4 against Mark Calcavecchia in the fifth game and Thomas Bjorn beat Stewart Cink 2 and 1. Europe had four and a half points from a possible 6, and at this point the strength of Torrance's gamble paid off, bringing the very best out of the supposedly weaker players.

The best performance of the lot came from Philip Price, of whose selection many had been critical. He looked so white and ashen that one theory was that he frightened Phil Mickelson to death simply by appearing on the first tee, but there was nothing pale about his golf as he defeated the world number two by 3 and 2. 'I didn't think I had it in me,' Price said later, 'but I'm glad to find I have.' His win left McGinley, another of the so-called also-rans, to curl a ten-foot putt into the centre of the hole and set European celebrations alight, while on the final green Parnevik had a four-footer to halve with Tiger. 'Jesper's fought hard all day. I wouldn't want to see him miss that,' said Woods as he picked up the ball to register half a point for each side.

Sam burst into tears, as expected, and kissed and hugged everyone in sight well into the night, pausing only for the odd pint or two. Curtis Strange insisted he was not unhappy with his line-up, but what else can you say in the circumstances?

Amanda Puts Jonathan Back on Course

Buick Challenge, Pine Mountain, 2002

I don't know anything about Amanda Talley, although in the photographs she looks like a very pleasant young woman, even if she is wincing slightly at the recurrent stabs of pain. She may love golf every bit as much as her fiancé, Jonathan Byrd, or she may detest the game and show up loyally just to give him her support. How she feels about it after the final round of the Buick Challenge, 2002, we can only conjecture. Bruised, for sure. Forgiving? Only Jonathan can really say.

The Buick Challenge is the penultimate tournament of the US season and Jonathan was doing pretty well as he came down the back nine in the final round. Full of the joys of vanishing fall and approaching winter, not to mention impending marriage to Amanda, he hurled himself into an overenthusiastic tee shot and could only watch in horror as the ball sliced wildly towards the distant pines. In among the trees the only possibility would be to play out sideways and that would mean an almost certain bogey six and the end of his lead. But Jonathan had reckoned without Amanda.

It wasn't exactly that she flung herself heroically into the path of the ball and headed it onto the green, but unbeknown to Jonathan, she was standing between the ball and the pines. He did, though, see his missile ricochet off a cart track, smack into a spectator and rebound into light rough on the way to the green. It was only as he drew near that he realised the victim was his beloved. But was he still her beloved? Did he seize her in his arms and kiss it better? Apparently not. 'Thanks,' he said with a somewhat sheepish grin, took out his 3-wood and struck the ball into the heart of the green before double-putting for a birdie four.

Amanda's sufferings were not in vain – at least as far as her fiancé was concerned. Jonathan finished with a nine-under-par round of 63 for an aggregate 261 and victory in the tournament by one stroke. Buoyed by the win that hoisted him to 41st in the American money list, Jonathan was in more expansive mood later when asked about the incident. 'She took it for the team,' he explained enigmatically, holding a golf umbrella over her head as protection against further stray projectiles. Before she went down the aisle a month later Amanda may have asked for a new clause in her marriage contract, requiring her new husband to win tournaments without using her as a bouncing board.

Mark Roe Becomes Acquainted With 6-6d

The Open, Royal St George's, 2003

The problems golfers have with their scorecards! Those crumpled little scraps of card that we haul into and out of our back pocket and cover with squiggles that we can't decipher at the end of the round have spent a hundred years and more causing trouble. But for the porridge the Americans made of their 2000 presidential election with machinery that was supposedly infallible, you'd think it was better to have an electronic system with a keyboard at each hole. Enter your score with your PIN, verified by your playing partner's PIN, and Bob's your uncle. Leader board instantly updated and no more messy problems in the scorer's hut at the end of the round. But let's get back to cold reality.

Mark Roe is not one of golf's best-known names on the circuit, but he's a more than decent player who, as he said himself, 'felt blessed in having nineteen wonderful years on tour – golf has been massively good to me.' In the 2003 Open at Royal St George's he was playing a blinder. Partnering Jesper Parnevik in the third round, he shot a brilliant 67 (two better than the 69 of Thomas Bjorn, who was looking the likely winner) to finish the day only two strokes short of the lead. Mark was understandably cheerful as he took the applause on the eighteenth green. He could look forward to being in contention in the final round and the near certainty of a big cheque at the end of it. He did not know that, at that very moment, rule 6-6d was preparing to pounce.

At the start of their round, Parnevik and Roe were handed two identical little squares of paper, their cards. The rules dictate that each player enter his name on the aforesaid card and hand it to his playing partner for each to keep the other's score. No cheating that way, all nice and above board. Alas and alack, our heroes forgot to exchange cards. They duly and accurately recorded the number of shots each took for every hole, added them all up and came to the right totals – a bothersome 81 for Mr Parnevik, dissociating him from further meaningful interest in the competition; an uplifting 67 for Mr Roe, 'the best day of his sporting life', as *The Times* commented. At which point the sky fell on his head, on both their heads, as the rules committee reached for its black cap and pronounced the sentence of doom – disqualification forthwith and immediate expulsion from the seaside resort of Sandwich.

There was much muttering and arm-waving among the assembled multitude of journalists and spectators. 'Inflexible', 'absurd', 'heartless' and suchlike comments filled the air – but none of them uttered by Mark Roe. The point was that Parnevik had, in effect, signed for a 67 when he took 81. No possible reprieve there. Roe, on the other hand, had effectively signed for 81 when he took 67, and if you sign your card for a score higher than the one you actually shot there is no penalty. The problem arose because, in signing the wrong card, Roe had also signed for Parnevik's four at the fourth hole, the one time he had taken more strokes (five) himself.

He was bitterly disappointed – he could hardly fail to be – but, as the messages of sympathy flooded in, he said, 'I had nobody to blame but myself. The rules and traditions of golf are what set the game apart. We call penalties on ourselves and accept it without question when we break the rules. Even if the R&A had found a way to reinstate me, I wouldn't have wanted to play. You accept what the game throws at you and get on with it.'

The grace and candour with which Roe swallowed his unhappiness put people in mind of another great sportsman in similar straits – Roberto de Vicenzo at the 1968 Masters (see page 78), and to be bracketed with such a man may be some small consolation.

The Sands of Sandwich

The Open, Royal St George's, 2003

Thomas Bjorn comes from Sweden, where any loose sand is tidied quickly out of sight, but for golfing purposes he is based in Dubai, where there is sand over and to spare. If your bunker play is keeping you awake at night, you have only to nip out to the back garden in your pyjamas and practise to your heart's content. One can think of many reasons why Bjorn might have fallen one stroke short of capturing his first major, but making a mess in the sand is not the first to spring to mind. But so, alas, it was and it did little to improve Thomas's near-legendary temper.

The ability to overheat his internal-combustion engine about something not to his liking had cost him dear right from the off. On Royal St George's seventeenth hole he had wound up in a bunker during the first round. On failing to get out of it at the first attempt, he slammed his wedge into the sand to teach it a lesson and seriously displeased the rules committee, who do not like to see defenceless clubs ill-used. They slapped a two-stroke penalty on him. In the event, that alone might have cost him a swig from the Claret Jug when it was all over had it not been for exemplary second and third rounds of 70 and 69 respectively, played in demure good humour. Suddenly, he was right back in contention. As he said, 'I can't look at the first round and say that cost me because every player had something happen to them over the four days.' All very true, but there are those things the fates inflict on you and those you bring down on yourself.

Bjorn's final round was a stormer – until he spotted a patch of sand on the sixteenth that unhinged him. As he came to the 163-yard par-three hole he was three under par for the round with a lead of two shots. One look at the bunker and the sirens of the sands called to him. He drove straight into it. As bunkers go, it was a moderately shallow, inoffensive little thing, at the foot of a slight rise to the green, nothing to cause too much concern. Thomas shuffled his feet, waggled his bottom and then his sand wedge and splashed out of the bunker with an impressive little chip to the flag. The ball reached the top of the slope, paused for reflection as it saw itself surrounded by cold green grass, and scurried back to the warmth of the sand.

Controlling his temper admirably, Thomas repeated the procedure as before, and so did the ball. 'It was', wrote one reporter, 'as if he was performing in an exhibition of trickery.' Third time lucky, he played the shot he had wanted all along, sank the putt and walked off, all clubs intact and in his bag, with a double-bogey five. His lead was gone, there were not enough holes left to recover the lost ground and Bjorn finished a stroke behind the hitherto unknown winner, Ben Curtis. No reporter was intrepid enough to follow Bjorn to see if he took his sand wedge round the back of the clubhouse for capital punishment.

Oh, You Are a Tease, You Really Are!

Johnnie Walker Classic, Bangkok, 2004

Just as there are some golfers whose disposition seems cloudlessly sunny, and who play with an expression of inane pleasure permanently imprinted on their faces (Phil Mickelson springs effortlessly to mind), there are others who will impersonate Vesuvius at the clatter of a club. Thomas Bjorn and Colin Montgomerie rank high on the list of those with volcanic temperaments. Bjorn may be a Swede, and therefore expected to conform to the ice-cold stereotype of his nation, but if things are not precisely so he is apt to take aim with both barrels, as Jyoti Randhawa discovered during the 2002 Hong Kong Open. Partnering Bjorn, Randhawa played his round with care or, to be more forthright, was very slow. Bjorn made his feelings so abundantly plain that a formal complaint of abuse was laid against him, to which his response was, 'I've had a problem for two days playing with you and you deserve to be abused.' No room for misunderstandings there.

Since Colin Montgomerie has also been known to get a bit agitated now and again, it came as little surprise when he and Thomas had a run-in during the second round of the Johnnie Walker Classic in Bangkok. Monty was feeling less than equable after plopping his ball into the water at the seventh hole, but in the meantime Bjorn was concentrating on a demanding chip from the rough onto the green. Just as he drew back his club there came the thunder of a minor cavalry charge on the bridge behind him as Monty crossed it. It was nothing like that in reality, of course, even though Monty is a big fellow, but that is evidently how it sounded to Bjorn.

Once again he felt it only right to leave no doubts about his opinion and to do so with the directness for which he is justly famed. Matters were not improved when he finally got back to his chip shot. It was a poor one, and he registered a bogey, so, when he completed his round, he complained to the match referee, notwithstanding he was in the lead at twelve under par.

Monty was far from amused. Indeed, he was positively perturbed. 'Come over here right now,' he demanded, generating an even greater volume of steam than Bjorn. If he had been wearing a jacket, he would probably have peeled it off there and then and limbered up with a spot of shadow boxing. Sensing it was time to step between them, the referee, Miguel Vidaor, bravely did so, and succeeded in ushering them into an enclosed space where they were free from the prying eyes of the press. Neither carried any visible scars when they emerged, so if there were injuries they were presumably internal. Indeed, they now seemed to be the best of friends. 'I did some things wrong, and Colin did some things wrong,' said Thomas making a late bid, as one reporter put it, for a run at the Nobel Peace Prize. 'We're as good friends as we were before we went out and we will always be good friends.' It all sounded disarmingly like one of those announcements made by Hollywood couples as they wrap themselves round each other a fortnight before filing for a divorce.